THE GREYSTONE'S NIGHTMARES

Francesco Cheynet & Lucio Schina

2023 All rights reserved to authors

Any duplicate in circulation or attempt to duplicate, violates the current copyright laws and may be prosecuted under the law.

The novel stems from the imagination of the authors and has no ambition of historical reconstruction. However, in writing it, the authors adhered to the customs and customs of the epochs in which it is set.

Copyright © 2023
Francesco Cheynet e Lucio Schina
www.schinacheynetlibri.it

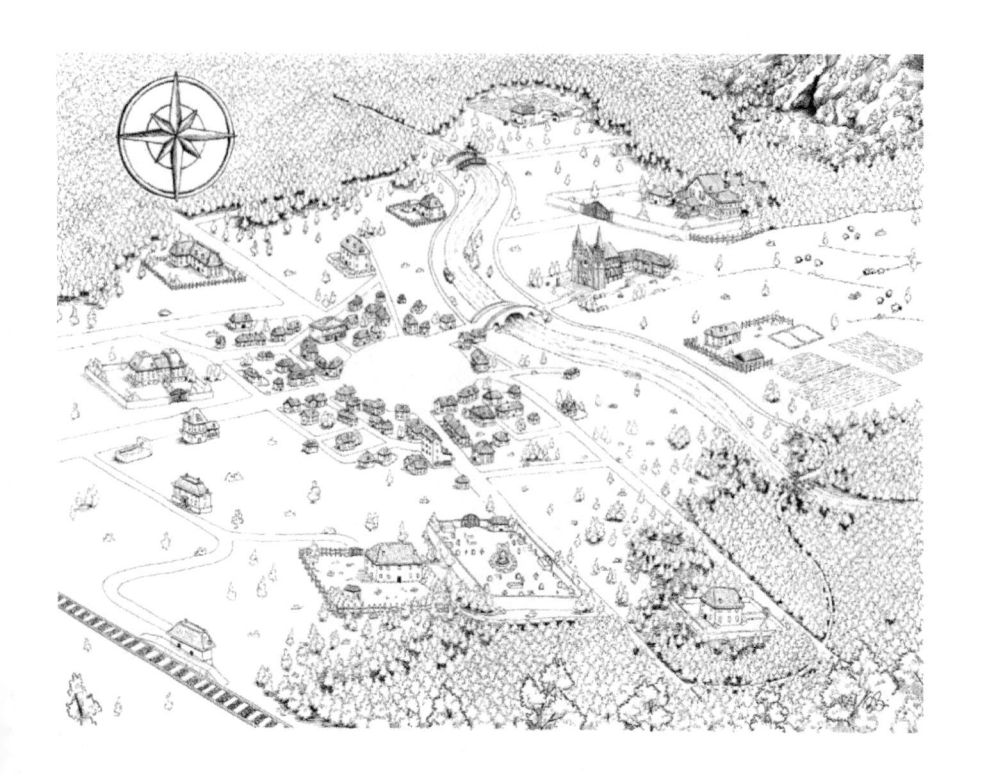

Greystone's map
by Venessa Barbiero

BACKGROUND

27 October 1750

The deacon passed through the entrance gate and came panting at the doorway. He turned to make sure that no one had followed him, then, adjusting his cloak and tricorn, he knocked violently on the door. When a servant opened the door, he asked to be announced to the master of the house.
'I have a letter to deliver to His Eminence Arthur William Harrington.'
'Who shall I announce?' Asked the man standing on the edge of the door.
The uniform gave him a ceremonial look; he wore knee-length velvet trousers with inlays on the edges, a white silk shirt with elaborate lapels, a waistcoat finished with arabesque motifs and a wig with silvery reflections. Elegant counter-shoulder straps adorned a long ruby-coloured jacket with large golden bell-shaped buttons.
'Bishop Matthews' deacon.'
While waiting to be received, the boy was intrigued by the notes of orchestral music coming from the reception hall. The evening of the grand ball showed itself in all its magnificence; sumptuously dressed couples danced in the centre of the hall, while at the sides the guests conversed, tasting the best wines from the master's personal reserve, accompanying them with delicious food arranged on long tables adorned with silk tablecloths with lace embroidered around the edges. The atmosphere was warmed by the logs burning inside a large fireplace in the north corner of

the room, whose majesty was embellished by a Greek Carrara marble that followed the contours.

The deacon looked up to admire the crystal chandeliers, which projected reflections of every colour of the rainbow onto the floor.

As usual, the villagers had been invited to celebrate the end of the harvest, which was very abundant that year. His face, however, betrayed a deep uneasiness. He held his cloak tightly to himself as if he had been tasked with protecting an object of great value. He walked away from the salon and made his way to the entrance. He cast a furtive glance outside; the evening was clear and starry. Although the calendar heralded the imminent arrival of winter, the temperature that year remained mild, but the deacon's hands trembled and he was shivering with cold. He closed the tent, moved away the cloak with one arm and checked the inside of the saddlebag. Some heavy steps made him almost jerk; he turned and looked in the direction of the corridor that opened to his right. From the bottom, the flickering light of a candle approached him, barely illuminating the faces of the ancient nobles of the house, framed and carefully arranged on the walls. The servant beckoned to follow him, turned around and, with the same martial procession, led him before a door.

'His Eminence is waiting for you,' he announced laconically.

The deacon thanked and entered, while the servant closed the door discreetly.

The room was illuminated by a lighted fireplace and the light of candelabra placed at the sides of a rectangular table that dominated the centre.

'Please forgive my visit, but I have been instructed to report this matter is of the utmost importance!' He cried out in fear in the presence of the rich lords, as he removed his tricorn and took a slight bow.

'You are a welcome guest tonight, so please take your seat and taste this liqueur...' Arthur William Harrington began in a jovial tone as he poured him half a cup.

'You're too good, Milord,' the boy said, grabbing it with both hands.

'The servant has informed me that you have an embassy to deliver to me; but first, let me introduce you to the guests here present: the county judge, Durward Owen, who has just arrived in our community, and the mayor Nickolas Chapman, who, on this jubilant evening, has honoured us with his visit. But am I mistaken or are you shivering with cold? Please stand by the fire and regain your strength.'

As he observed the deacon's frightened gaze, Arthur William's chubby face changed in expression, as if caught by a bad omen. He poured some rum and sat back down taking off his wig.

'Are you here on behalf of the bishop?'

'No Milord, His Eminence is unaware of this matter. Sheriff Harvey sent me.'

The young man's sharp, black eyes scrutinized Sir Arthur William's questions while waiting for an explicit nod.

'You may therefore speak freely, the gentlemen here present enjoy the utmost confidence.'

With a quick gesture, the deacon swallowed the rum all in one sip, placed the chalice on a wall desk and widened his cloak until he got rid of it. He opened the saddlebag and took out a sealed wax letter.

'Forgive me, my lord, but the Sheriff has expressed the wish that you open it in my presence and do not delay reading it for any reason.'

Arthur William Harrington took the letter in his hand. He put on a pair of prescription lenses, approached a candelabra, and opened the yellow envelope, reading the contents in a low voice. The mayor Chapman and judge Owen had stood by and watched without intervening. Their faces, cheerful only a few minutes earlier, now appeared concerned.

'Gentlemen!' Arthur William Harrington exclaimed after folding the letter and taking off his lenses, 'Sheriff Harvey has just consulted Madame Althea; the dogs are howling in the sky and the mountain has begun to tremble. I have to inform you reluctantly that the beast is lending itself to return.'

21 October 1884 – Tuesday

Winter had arrived well in advance that year, bringing a cold and heavy snowfall. The inns' signs fluttered in sudden gusts of wind; tall columns of grey smoke rose from the chimneys of the houses and their slopes seemed to collapse under the thick layer of snow. Few people could be seen walking in the streets, and the muffled silence was interrupted only by the shouting of the children, who played at chasing each other and throwing snowballs. The white landscape and the crisp air gave the village an almost mystical aura.

Climbing up the street that cuts it in two from south to north, once you passed St Patrick Square and the Ducks Bridge, an old bridge of medieval origin, you reached the local church. It was an ancient Gothic style building, built around the 13th century using the perimeter of an early Christian sanctuary, whose remains still emerged along the west side in the form of dry stone walls.

The vast cultivable expanses of land guaranteed work and food for the entire population; thanks to the use of advanced agricultural techniques, high productivity made it possible to accumulate large surpluses of products, which were stored and then sold in the markets thanks to the goods trains that passed through the local station on a daily basis. The river water shone in the sun and swarmed with every species of fish, as well as being an inexhaustible source during the irrigation of the fields. If a stranger had found himself passing through the village, he could have described it as a small paradise out of the fertile imagination of a novelist, a fairy tale place purified by the white cloak that was deposited there. But from the bowels of the depths a scarlet spot was preparing to infect the earth, spreading its seeds like a plague and turning the sense of harmony into a mad maze of violence.

Vernon Doyle had anticipated his arrival at the church many hours earlier that day. Darkness still reigned and he had already finished arranging the books left on the tables. He had gone to the entrance of the church making sure the door was locked. Returning to the library, after having moved one of the desks and rolled up the carpet on which it rested, he found the tile with a small cross engraved on it; he lifted it together with the two adjacent ones, bringing to light a hollow bay. From the inside, he pulled out a leather document holder that held an ancient text preserved in excellent condition. He scrolled through the pages until he found the one he was looking for, after which he carefully laid it on the table, spreading his arms and beginning to whisper strange verses written in Celtic. When he felt a slight vibration under the floor, he gave the voice a deeper tone, repeating the formula mechanically until it plunged into a state of paroxysmal tension. The sinister rumble of thunder broke the silence of the room, while the dim light of the moon coming in through the windows died under the weight of a shapeless mantle of grey clouds coming from nowhere, which plunged the village into a spectral darkness. Terrified by the uncontrollable consequences that the celebration of the rite was causing, Vernon Doyle grabbed the crucifix he was holding around his neck, squeezing it so tightly that he made deep cuts in the palm of his hand. In a few seconds, the sacred object began to stain itself with the blood coming out of the wounds, creating a dense rivulet that ended up dripping on the ground following the contours of the figure of Christ. He ignored the meaning of the formula but knew that among the folds of time hid an entity that would guarantee immortality to those who would be able to evoke it and secure its favour, once awakened and pushed to abandon its dwelling in the underworld. The low clouds had wrapped the church in an icy grip and the lashing wind made the window shutters tremble. An ominous darkness limited visibility to a few steps and brought with it the sweet smell of death.

Vernon Doyle closed the book in terror and hid it in its place, then ran out of the library and knelt in front of the large wooden crucifix behind the altar. He began to invoke the Lord's forgiveness by using a flap of his shirt to cleanse the sacred image from his now infected blood. The trembling of his hands became so frenetic that he began to feel painful pains, until the horror of what was evoked took hold of him until he cried out in despair. It was a moment when his voice strangled in his throat. Vernon Doyle did not understand what was happening to him; swallowed in a vortex of delirious images he began to feel a slight warmth in the centre of his chest, a sensation that descended on his belly and ended wet between his legs. His eyes grainy were on the verge of splashing out of their sockets. When the crucifix slipped on the floor he only had the strength to raise one hand and carry it around his neck. A hot, sticky liquid gushed from a deep wound that opened under his jaw, a tear so wide that his head bent back unnaturally. Vernon Doyle tried to block the blood flow by dabbing it with the palm of his hand, but it slid inward until it touched the cervical bones. A stabbing pain spread along the sensitive nerves of the body, while the colour of the face became funereal. He moved back a few steps, staring at a shadow that was approaching threateningly. The blurred vision prevented him from focusing on the beast, but he could see the outline of a huge figure with goat's horns sticking out of its skull like infected pustules. Its hands, bony and deformed, held sharp blades dripping blood, his blood, which the creature demanded as a sacrifice to its glory. It made a moan like a funeral lament, its eyes blackened and its mouth contracted into a fierce grin. When it reached the front, almost without essence, it went through him from side to side with its body, vaporizing the next instant. Vernon Doyle had a gasp before breathing his last breath; two large gashes had opened his belly wide open and caused his bowels to spill out, which blurred on the floor into a lake of blood.

20 October 1884 – Monday

From the window of his office Dorian Bayley watched with his mind elsewhere the carriages parked opposite the entrance to Scotland Yard. He had only started his shift ten minutes earlier, but he was still enjoying a cigar and was happily losing himself in thoughts that ranged far in time and space. That morning he was thinking back to the times he had been assigned to that office. At that time, the carriages were counted on the fingers of one hand and the owners were well known within the department.

At half past seven in the morning, with a light fog still veiling the city, London was experiencing a sleepy awakening; the pace at which the world as turning suggested to Dorian Bayley that he should take a few moments before throwing himself headlong into the investigations left unresolved. As punctual as clockwork Emily Clarke, the secretary in charge of sorting the internal mail and reception, knocked on the door and, without waiting for a reply, came in with a steaming cup of tea and a handwritten note.

'What would I do without you?' asked the inspector grabbing his cup of tea and enjoying the warmth on his hands.

'I suppose your wife could look after you and make you a nice cup of tea,' replied the secretary with a nice smile.

Dorian Bayley had thick graying hair that tended, year after year, towards white. He was taller than average and, despite his age, in a few months he would have turned fifty, he kept in full physical shape. His dark eyes showed a vivid, bright look, but sometimes his pupils pointed in an abstract direction as if he was wandering with his mind in a distant and impenetrable galaxy. It was at times when he seemed absent that his intuition suggested details that could lead him to the resolution of a case. A sort of superior intuition that belonged to his own being, an innate dowry and not the fruit of the close training that had led him to become an inspector.

'What's that in your hand, an invitation to the theatre?' He asked ironically while quietly sipping tea.

'Sorry, but Paul Carter, your boss, gave me this!' Emily specified.

Paul Carter was the Chief Inspector of the Investigation Department, the most important figure within Scotland Yard.

'Carter decided to get up early in the morning,' muttered Dorian.

He took the note from the secretary's hands and read it while imagining its contents. It was written on it:

'As soon as you have a minute, show up at my office.'

He raised his eyes to the ceiling fearing a huge annoyance. On the other hand, when it came to ordinary cases, Carter had the files to study delivered directly to him; when something delicate was at stake, however, he summoned the inspectors to his office to anticipate them by voice.

'Good luck!' Emily wished, greeting as she walked out the door.

Five minutes later Dorian Bayley was sitting opposite Paul Carter, with his forearms resting along the edge of the desk.

'What's this about?' He nipped any convention in the bud.

'*Greystone!* Do you know where it is?' Carter answered, staring him in the eye.

'I must have heard it before...but offhand I can't remember.'

'Northern England,' continued the Chief Inspector. 'It's a small village of no more than 500 souls; a small, wealthy community nestled between the hills and nowhere, about 550 miles from here.'

'A paradise, therefore,' commented Dorian Bayley. 'Is this a prize trip to celebrate 30 years of service at Scotland Yard?'

'Not exactly Dorian, but I thought you might like to get away from London a bit.'

'Tell me about the case.'

'There's been a theft inside a house; it's an ancient text, something to do with magic and spiritualism.'

Dorian Bayley couldn't hold back a laugh.

'You're asking me to take a day and a half of traveling for the theft a book about witches and sorcerers?'

Carter huffed; he anticipated that objection and kept the second part of the story to himself. He shook his head and started talking again.

'Of course not! The village, although small, is of some importance to the county's economy, as it exports its crops to all nearby markets, including feed for farm animals. Considering it a strategic area, the government, also at the request of the mayor, several years ago pressured Scotland Yard to send its own officer to coordinate a small police station consisting of three policemen, who exchange shifts to ensure safety.'

The Chief Inspector paused to give Dorian Bayley a chance to point out to him that, for an event of that magnitude, an officer from Scotland Yard was more than enough. But this time Dorian didn't bite and waited for the Chief Inspector to speak again.

'The problem is this; our officer disappeared five days after the theft and since then, no one has heard from him.'

'Who is it?' Churches intrigued.

'The Inspector Nevil Morgan. '

'Nevil Morgan?' Dorian said to his amazement, 'The enigmatic Nevil, the one who solved cases by invoking the name of the guilty party in a dream?'

This time it was Carter who couldn't hold back a laugh.

'That's the one.'

'I haven't seen him for at least fifteen years...' he continued, reflecting '...we had attended a refresher session and that's when I got to know him. An out-of-the-ordinary character, a completely original type. He once told me he'd tracked down a missing person through a séance. I've never met anyone like him in my entire life.'

'Now he's the one who's missing, and I have to admit, I'm worried about that.' Carter regained a serious expression. 'He's a bit eccentric and we agree on that, but he's a great guy and he's never been a problem at work.'

Dorian Bayley tried to return with his mind to the present and his expression became pensive.

'When should I leave?'

'This afternoon at two o'clock; here in this envelope are the tickets. From London a train will take you to Middlesbrough and there you will sleep at *The House* Hotel, located just outside the station. In the morning at seven o'clock you will take a steamer that will drop you off at *Greystone* Station, where a local agent will pick you up. You are expected to arrive around nine.' Said the Chief Inspector.

'You just assumed I'd say yes.' Dorian Bayley observed vexed.

'That's right!' Carter replied with a narrow-lipped smile, 'in the indoor parking lot you have a carriage with a coachman who will drive you home and then to the train station. Warn your wife and tell her you don't know how many days you'll be staying. If in doubt, bring the necessary for at least two weeks.'

'I suppose I'll have to ask the officer I'll find on arrival for the accommodation.'

'We've already thought about that; you'll stay in the room of an inn surrounded by greenery so you can concentrate, with a great view of the surrounding hills.'

Dorian Bayley did not answer; the assignment intrigued him and Carter was not wrong about it. He knew his boss all too well and, although he appeared to be demanding and grumpy, he knew his job. In assigning cases, he not only evaluated the state of service but also considered personal expectations.

'Hand me the file,' he said pretending he'd thought about it.

'Here we are! Everything's inside!' Carter exclaimed, pushing some badly bound sheets of paper that were lying on the desk towards him.

'Perfect! See you when I get back.'

Dorian Bayley walked to the door; when he opened it he heard Carter's voice again.

'Dorian!'

The inspector turned around.

'I have a feeling it's not going to be a vacation. I hope I'm wrong.'

Dorian Bayley closed the door without following up those words and headed for the exit.

21 October 1884 – Tuesday

Taking advantage of the lukewarm sun and a weather that seemed to be turning to beauty, that morning Joseph Beathan decided to reach the church by changing the route he used to follow. After three days in which it had done nothing but snow, he thought that the best thing was to breathe the pure air of the woods.
He ate his usual breakfast, prepared himself quickly and left the house; he stopped for a few minutes at the Wilson's, who lived across the street and to whom years earlier he had donated a piece of land transformed over time into a vegetable garden. He wanted to thank Mrs Wilson for the apple pie she had prepared the day before and, above all, to say hello to little Emma; a four-year-old girl who did nothing but smile and with whom he was in love as the most affectionate of fathers.
'See you Sunday at church.' He took his leave after returning the plate.
Since he had been sent to *Greystone* to run St Patrick's Church, Father Beathan had managed to enter into the sympathies of the inhabitants, who now considered him a spiritual figure of reference. A reserved temperament and an innate aversion to political disquisition had prevented him from accepting the invitation to become a member of the local council, even though he intervened publicly whenever questions of solidarity and sharing out the surplus crop to those most in need were to be discussed. He never failed to give a smile or a greeting to the people he met and he always ended the discussions by making an appointment for the following Sunday's service. His

prayers had won the favour of the faithful and within a few years, he had managed to return the church to the centre of social life in the country, overcoming the harmful effects of famine and corrupt priests that had resulted in degrading the reputation of any man who professed to be an intermediary of God. The church had thus ceased to be a place to avoid and had returned to play the role of a second home, ready to extend its hand to its faithful.

The path in the wood, which had only been cleared the day before, had once again been covered by a thick layer of snow that had fallen just before the day began. Father Beathan lifted his black habit by tying it to his knees and continued the walk with a branch broken by snow, which he used as an improvised walking stick. He limped with his left-handed leg but was able to hide the defect thanks to his slender build and strong gait.

After about half an hour he reached the edge of the forest; from there he climbed up along the path that came out on the main road just before the Ducks Bridge. It was the time when the village began to come to life and Father Beathan accelerated his pace to arrive on time. When he arrived near the portico, he noticed the door still closed. He climbed the three wooden steps and struck the ring door with force; the caretaker, Vernon Doyle, had the task of opening it at about seven thirty, after having arranged the library and tidied up the sacristy, and he used to arrive before dawn to complete his assigned tasks, an operation he had been repeating with laborious regularity every morning for almost thirteen years.

Not receiving an answer, the priest tried to ring the bell, so he went around and went to the back. He reached the door of the library, a huge 'L' shaped room built as an extension of the church, from which one could access the sacristy through an internal corridor.

He turned the handle with a slight pressure with his shoulder, but found this door locked as well. He thought for a moment what to do and then decided to look for him in his house. He stepped out of the garden, walked over the Ducks Bridge and into St Patrick's Square, took a dead-end alleyway that opened into the centre of the square to the east. He asked the neighbours, one of whom confirmed that he heard Vernon Doyle leaving the house just before four o'clock.

'Why so early? God forbid something happened to him!' He exclaimed making the sign of the cross.

The deacon, who in the meantime had reached him in a hurry after passing through the church, stopped in front of him.

'Father... Perhaps we should call George Davies, the blacksmith,' he suggested, panting.

'It's a good idea Edward, on the way back, go and tell the police too; I'll wait for you there.' He answered hopefully.

When Edward arrived a few minutes later in the company of the two men, they found Father Beathan insisting on knocking and calling out Vernon Doyle's name.

'Father,' the young officer began, 'the deacon informed me on the way here. Inspector Morgan is currently untraceable. The best thing to do is to open the door and check that everything inside is in order. Then we'll send out a missing person's report.'

'Please,' replied the priest, leaving room for the blacksmith while he dried his maddening forehead with a handkerchief.

George Davies asked those present to come down the steps and move over the porch; he laid the heavy toolbox on the ground, pulled out some elements and started working by bending over the lock.

'Can you tell me when was the last time you saw Vernon Doyle?' The officer asked opening a notebook and taking a pencil out of his pocket. His name was Jacob Young and he'd been employed by Inspector Nevil Morgan for no more than three years.

'Last night around 7:00; I remember saying good-bye to him before I left the church to go home. I assume he stayed about eight o'clock, as usual. He's supposed to close before 8:30 and reopen at 7:30 in the morning.'

'Don't you have the keys with you?'

'I never take them, that's what Vernon always thinks. He always has a bunch of them while the second one is in the sacristy and we only use it in case of need. That I remember has never been used by anyone.'

The deacon confirmed Father Beathan's words, adding, however, that in recent times Vernon Doyle was more reserved than usual.

'Did he have any problems that you know of?'

'Vernon lives alone in the village and everyone loves him. He has a sister in London who, however, he rarely sees. He's a gentle, simple man. I can't think of a reason why he'd want to leave the church,' replied the priest.

A noise of hinges breaking interrupted the conversation. George Davies put the tools in the box, stood up and gave a vigorous push to the door, which opened inwards, dropping the key left in the keyhole. Then he waved goodbye and walked towards the village.

'This way...' Father Beathan led the way.

The young policeman beckoned the two of them to wait for his order. He put his notebook and pencil in a jacket pocket, took out his truncheon and entered with caution. From the outside you could hear the sound of footsteps getting weaker and weaker until they disappeared completely.

A few minutes later, which seemed like an eternity to Father Beathan, you could hear the steps of the policeman approaching with breathless breath. From the nervous pace he seemed to be fleeing; he came out slamming the door behind him with force. He leaned his back against the door, spreading his arms and bending his knees as if to prevent someone from getting out. His face was bleached and his green eyes were filled with terror. He took off his helmet and ran his hand through his hair, then stopped by a flowerbed and started vomiting as he bent forward.
'My God, it's terrible, terrible!' He had only the strength to exclaim.
'What happened, son?' He asked in a frightened tone Father Beathan as he tried to comfort him by patting him on the shoulder.
'We need to close the church and cordon off the area,' replied the policeman, coughing, 'a horrible murder has just taken place in there.'

***

The train departing from Middlesbrough was used for freight transport, to which two passenger carriages equipped with wooden chairs had been added in the queue. When Dorian Bayley had found a seat there, he was already feeling tired by the long journey of the day before and a night in which he had struggled to sleep. As if that wasn't enough, he had arrived at the station more than an hour before the gates opened and had to wait 40 minutes standing up in the cold.
He had devoted the previous day's journey from London to Middlesbrough to the study of the files. The train had made more stops than he had imagined, and instead of going inland, which he knew was the shortest, it had

passed along the east coast, passing through places never heard of before, such as Boston, Skegness and Scunthorpe.

From the report read carefully several times, no significant clues emerged that suggested a starting point and a direction to follow. The book had been stolen from the home of Adam Ford on 13 October, a municipal officer responsible for the management and maintenance of the local cemetery. He was a man who had never given a chance to make people talk about himself, even though he had a irascible temper and lived in a house on the south-eastern outskirts of *Greystone*, just where the houses gave way to a large conifer forest. He was 56 years old and lived with his wife Olivia, almost ten years older. Their only son, Martin, had moved to Liverpool, where he had worked for over five years. In relation to the contents of the stolen book, the details provided did not go beyond those communicated verbally by the Chief Inspector; it was an esoteric manuscript. The author had hid behind the pseudonym *Ambactus Danu*, perhaps to escape persecution by the Inquisition courts.

The most delicate part of the whole story, however, was undoubtedly the disappearance of Nevil Morgan, the inspector in charge of the investigation. His blurred image had passed before his eyes for the entire night spent in his hotel room in Middlesbrough. He had not been able to focus on his physical appearance when he had met him in London, but fifteen years had passed and it seemed normal that he had not kept a vivid memory of his face. He remembered him short and strong, with a conspicuous receding hairline and an enigmatic look. That was all. There was nothing to link the theft of the book to his disappearance, but Dorian Bayley was wary of coincidences and was convinced that something would soon turn up. He remembered his colleague's passion for magic, séances and parapsychological phenomena. There had to be a connection, but the dynamics remained unknown for the moment.

The last person to see Inspector Morgan was Frank Owen. According to the file, Owen was the county judge, a role that belonged, before him, to his entire male lineage. He was an influential figure who was also respected for his strong personality. Of course, he had close professional relationships with Nevil Morgan, although they often met to discuss private matters. On the morning of 18 October, Inspector Morgan visited him in his home; the housekeeper, named Margaret, welcomed him as usual. She had sat him down in the reception room where, together with the judge, they had had a cup of tea and discussed for about twenty minutes; after leaving the villa, he had disappeared into thin air.

The slow pace of the train allowed Dorian Bayley to see through the window a perfect snowy landscape of white expanses and small groups of houses with floured roofs. At times the train was jumping, as if the rails were not well levelled, causing sudden jolts that made the journey even more stressful.

Before coming to *Greystone* he tried to rearrange chronologically the information contained in the dossier, which he had repeatedly taken in hand as if he wanted to fix in his mind some details that he thought were interesting.

On the evening of 13 October, a book was stolen from the home of Adam Ford, who had gone in person to report the incident to the police. On 18 October, in the morning, Nevil Morgan disappeared after visiting Judge Frank Owen. It was necessary to understand what had happened in that five-day interval, if the inspector had discovered something, who he had talked to, where he was with the case and if, at that moment, he was dealing with other investigations that could jeopardize his safety.

'It will be necessary to start from the home of Nevil Morgan,' he thought with conviction, aware of the importance of writing down every element that emerged, adding his own personal considerations.

When a small village made up of low stone buildings surrounded by snow took shape in the distance, the locomotive began to lose power and the wheels returned an annoying whistle. A wooden canopy, from which hung a sign with the name of the station engraved on it, welcomed Dorian Bayley, who packed his suitcase and put on his coat. He lifted the heavy luggage, approached the door and went down the stairs, taking care not to slip. On the right he noticed a man in uniform; he breathed in a breath of cold air that cleared his lungs and was astonished to feel overwhelmed by a burst of enthusiasm. He found himself forced to admit that Paul Carter was right again.

'Pleased to meet you, Inspector Bayley, my name is Jacob Young.' The policeman who approached him at a slow but steady pace introduced himself. 'I welcome you to *Greystone* on behalf of my colleagues as well. Your reputation precedes you and we are honoured to make your acquaintance. We are certain you will shed light on Inspector Morgan's disappearance.'

For officers from a small village in the north of England, being able to work with inspectors sent from London was an exceptional event. Since the arrival of Nevil Morgan, now considered a local, no Scotland Yard inspector had set foot in *Greystone,* let alone one who enjoyed the honours of being considered one of the best in the investigation department.

'Pleased to meet Jacob,' Bayley replied, 'if you could accompany me to my quarters I would arrange and store my things. Then we can start the investigation.'
'There's a problem, Inspector. I must inform you that we have just found the mutilated corpse of a man. He's the church librarian and caretaker named Vernon Doyle.'
Bayley noticed a shadow of terror in Jacob Young's expression. It was clear that no one there was accustomed to such ferocity and that in the eyes of the policeman there was an image that he would never forget.
'Where was the body found?'
'Inside the church, next to the altar.'
Dorian Bayley paused to reflect; the only rational thought he could formulate concerned the complexity of the case, which, it was now established, was much more complex than expected.
'Let's go to the inn, put your luggage down and, if you agree, I'll take you to inspect the crime scene that I shut down, leaving an officer on watch.'
'Sounds like a good idea,' confirmed the inspector, who politely rejected the officer's attempt to carry his luggage.

***

In the forecourt in front of the church a small group of curious people had already formed, informed of what had happened within a few minutes. Another policeman, who had been called out of duty hours, had the task of keeping them away from the entrance but, in fact, his intervention was limited to remaining motionless at the foot of the porch. At the sight of his colleague and the inspector, the policeman unhooked the stirrup holding the door and opened just enough to let them both in, then slipped inside and closed it behind them.

Dorian Bayley felt like he'd been thrown into hell. The beauty of the country, the pure air he breathed and that impression of absolute tranquillity had suddenly been supplanted by a lifeless body, victim of unprecedented violence. After a moment of bewilderment, he took the notebook and began to note down every detail, turning around the corpse with extreme caution. The spectacle was gruesome; the clothes at stomach level were torn and the belly ripped by two large parallel cuts that had caused the bowels to spill. Jacob Young kept his eyes fixed on Vernon Doyle's feet, trying to hide his discomfort from the inspector. At the carotid artery, a stab had been inflicted that had almost severed the head, which was bent to the right; from the depth of the cut, the inspector understood that the blow had been delivered with a brutal, almost superhuman force. On the palms of his hands there were cuts that were incompatible with an attempt to defend himself against short distance cuts. A chain with a crucifix lay beside the supine body; it was a small gold-plated object used by the faithful during the celebration of group prayers.

The sun filtered through the large windows that covered the entire perimeter walls of the church, projecting its rays close to the tormented body. The natural lighting was sufficient to make every corner of the church clear, except for the small side aisles that remained in the half-light and needed artificial light produced by large candelabra placed on both sides. The inspector noted that Vernon Doyle had had time to replace the worn candles and insert new ones with white wicks. After he looked up and studied the way the light filtered through the windows, he walked slowly around the corpse, staring at it as if waiting for something. Jacob Young stood by and watched fascinated the way his new boss had immersed himself in the case.

When he thought he had finished his preliminary analysis, the inspector noticed a tiny fragment shining just below the victim's elbow. He knelt down to pick it up, placed it in the palm of his hand and watched it carefully. It was a golden fragment no larger than a fingernail; he had to wear glasses to understand that the object reproduced the Greek letter 'Ω'. He carefully wrapped it in a handkerchief holding it open on the palm of his hand.
'Does this ring a bell?' He turned around and showed it to the two officers.
Jacob Young appeared to have been astonished; on the day he was assigned to *Greystone* he had rejoiced at the idea of serving in one of the quietest places in the county, the only country in the north of England which, although it had less than 500 inhabitants, had its own police station with an inspector, three officers and a judge, capable of providing an efficient police force with great deterrent power. *Greystone* had often risen to the headlines as one of the safest places in England, with a crime level close to zero. But the discovery of the corpse of Vernon Doyle, whom he knew personally even though he had never visited him, had awakened him from the dream of a paid stay, to throw him into the harsh awareness of a reality that had suddenly become mysterious and evil.
'Says nothing to me,' rests the second policeman who seemed most present and comfortable at the scene. Unlike his colleague, he had undertaken to inspect the body and the surrounding area for clues.
Jacob turned to look at the object the inspector was pointing at; he reflected for a moment, then shook his head.
Once closed the notebook, Dorian Bayley crossed a side aisle and entered the sacristy. On the left, on a cabinet, a wooden bowl contained a bunch of keys; on each one was

engraved a number and a sheet fixed to the wall indicated the corresponding room. At the end he noticed a couple of details that intrigued him. A chair lay on the floor about one from the table, towards the corridor. Next to it, as if it had fallen out of someone's hands, was a kerosene lamp with fragments of glass scattered on the floor. He left everything where it was and continued on to the library. Inside some curtains were drawn and the room was in half-light; he opened a couple of them and the light flooded the room like a flood wave. He made a complete tour looking for possible out-of-place objects, but all the books were impeccably arranged, as were the desks, arranged lengthways in two parallel rows, each of them resting on a red carpet, a chromatic nuance that tastefully echoed the colour of the curtains. When he reached the opposite end, he went back to wearing his glasses; he approached the front shelf, bending down almost to touch a shelf with his nose where fragments were deposited. With his thumb and index finger he rubbed a grassy residue; he carried his fingers under his nostrils and closed his eyes to develop his sense of smell to the maximum. Finally, he took a second handkerchief and collected the substance by dusting the shelf with one hand; it would have required a detailed analysis that could not be obtained on the spot.

'Jacob!' He called the inspector once back at the church, 'on the way here you told me that the priest found the door locked from the inside; can you confirm that?'

'Yes, of course! That's right! Both the library door and the church door.'

'And who opened it?'

'It was George Davies, the blacksmith...' replied the officer, who was slowly regaining colour, '...we went to call him together with the deacon, who had come to the police

station to warn me that this morning Vernon Doyle had not opened the church.'
'Is the blacksmith outside?'
'No! He came home as soon as he could blow the hinges.'
'Didn't he come in to check?'
'As soon as he unlocked the door he said goodbye and left in a hurry. Would you like me to check if he's home and have him come in?'
'No need. Let's go look for him together.'
Dorian Bayley wrapped the shard of gold in a handkerchief, put it in his pocket and turned to the second policeman.
'You keep everyone out and check if there are any more clues, but first carefully inspect the library. If we're lucky, you should find a chalice or a glass. Then come back here, pick up the crucifix and...' his gaze settled in the middle of the nave, about two steps beyond the victim's body in the direction of the altar '...those remnants of earth you see there.'
The inspector and Jacob left the church and found the priest just outside the door waiting for them; his face was the perfect portrait of anxiety.
'Father...if you have the patience to wait for me, I'll be back in an hour.' said Dorian Bayley.
'Could I enter the sacristy?' He asked quietly.
'At the moment, unfortunately, the church is being seized for the relief of the case. We will shortly have the body removed, after which you will be able to access it again.'
The priest spread his arms and nodded in passive approval.
Dorian Bayley beckoned the policeman to show him the way and they walked towards the centre of the village.

***

The blacksmith lived in a house in a building complex, just south of St. Patrick's Square, at the end of a wide street along the river. It was a modest building, with a storage room used as a laboratory. All around there was a small garden, which was accessed through an open gate.

As Jacob Young prepared to knock, hammer blows were heard coming from the lab. The inspector turned and beckoned his assistant to follow him. When they looked out of the half-open wooden door, they saw the man with his back to beat a piece of iron on an anvil. They waited for the hammering to stop, and when the blacksmith stopped to consider the partial result of his work, Jacob called him.

'Hi Jacob!' He greeted turning around and putting the big thing down on a shelf. Although the morning air was freezing cold, the effort to shape the iron plate had covered his forehead with sweat, from which large drops were dripping into a long, thick, dark beard. He was burly and tall, with powerful arms, a perfect example of a man skilled in manual labour, who used his strength to earn a living.

'This is Inspector Dorian Bayley from Scotland Yard; he'll be handling the case and wanted to ask you a few questions.'

'Good morning, Inspector. Welcome to *Greystone.*' the blacksmith greeted with a bow and wiped the sweat off his shirt sleeve.

'Good morning, you're very busy, so I'll only bother you for a moment.' the inspector said before taking a break.

'This morning you were called to force the front door of St. Patrick's Church as the priest...', and that's when Inspector Bayley realized he couldn't remember the name.

'Joseph Beathan.' Jacob came to his rescue.

The inspector thanked him with a nod of his head, then went on, 'Father Beathan I was saying, he was locked out, can you confirm that the door was locked?'
'Yes! It was locked from the inside; the key had been left in the keyhole and fell to the floor when I forced it with a shovel,' he replied confident.
'I can confirm that's what happened! As soon as I entered I saw the key on the floor behind the door; I picked it up and kept it in my pocket.' Jacob intervened.
The inspector looked George Davies in the eye again.
'Did you enter the church after opening it?'
'No! I came straight away.'
The inspector noticed that his interlocutor was of few words.
'May I ask why?'
George Davies lifted the iron plate in his hand and showed it to those present.
'I have to deliver it by this morning,' he simply added.
'One last question; have you seen anyone hanging around outside the church at times when no mass is said?'
George Davies reflected for a moment.
'Yes, two days ago, at sunset. A man dressed in a strange way, with a long dark cloak, went back and forth between the bridge and the garden. He first approached the main gate, then retraced his steps and headed towards the library. He peeked a couple of times inside, as if waiting for someone to arrive. He was walking with a walking stick, which is rare in these parts.'
The inspector and the policeman took one look at each other.
'Had you ever seen him before?'
'He was a stranger, I'm sure of that, but I was distant and I couldn't see his face. I couldn't even describe him. I was on my way to help an elderly woman who had been locked

in the house with the lock locked and I wanted to get there as soon as possible.'

'I understand, thank you for the information,' concluded Dorian Bayley as he wrote it all down in his notebook, then said goodbye before heading out.

Before inspecting Nevil Morgan's house, the inspector decided to return to the crime scene to make sure the coroner had been called in to examine the body before it was transported to the cemetery morgue. He had time to talk to the deacon and the priest who merely confirmed what he already knew. Vernon Doyle was 37, and born and raised in *Greystone*. He had never met his father, who moved to Australia for work when he was two years old and over time had lost track of him until he disappeared completely, but his mother had died of tuberculosis leaving him an orphan at sixteen. Father Beathan took care of him, welcomed him into the house and raised him as a son, finally giving him the chance to work as a librarian. In the village he was well-liked and had no enemies; an existence marked by the pain of loss but similar to that of many others. He possessed no riches of any kind, yet someone had brutally murdered him, plotting a seemingly perfect and, in some respects, inexplicable murder. At the scene of the crime there were no obvious traces of foreign presence; the two doors were locked from the inside and the motive could not be of an economic nature. Even stranger still, the inspector thought, the murderer had not abandoned the murder weapon but had chosen to take it with him, running the slight risk of phases noted during the escape. The only reason, he concluded, was that the weapon itself could be recognizable and, therefore, lead back to its owner.

Inspector Morgan's notes could have given him additional clues, giving him a chance to focus his attention on a possible lead. He decided to look for them first in his office and then in his home. He followed the officer to the police station, which was near the train station just to the east. It was a building originally built for a different use; the entrance hall was actually a small rounded space created after removing two side walls, traces of which were still visible on the floor. A short corridor led into a central room, where there was a blackboard, a desk, a wood-burning stove and no windows; the entrance door had been unhinged and immediately to the right, a hook held a red bucket full of water, with a plaque next to it on which was written *"firefighting system"*. Two side doors, with frosted glass at the top, led to two private offices. The one on the left, as the name printed on the glass, belonged to Inspector Morgan.

Dorian Bayley opened the door to what would be his office; the environment was small but rather cosy. Next to the window, overlooking the back, there was a bare desk with only an oil lamp resting on it, next to a coat rack two chairs supported piles of stacked briefcases, while on the walls several wooden shelves were filled with classified documents and books of various kinds. In the corner near the desk, on the right, a wood-burning stove seemed to have been unused for some time, even though there was a stack of wooden logs forming a small pyramid on the side. The commissioner waited for the second policeman, whose name he still didn't know, to come back and give him the doctor's preliminary report. After remaining motionless in the middle of the room to familiarize himself with the new environment, he sat down looking for a comfortable position, put his notes in order and wrote them down on a sheet of paper on which he put the date and name of the missing inspector. Once the operation was over, he got up and opened the window, took a metal cigar case from his jacket pocket; he chose a cigar at random and lit it contemplating the panorama of the snowy woods in silence.

Two hours later there was a knock on the door, Jacob stood on the edge informing him that officer Gordon Craig had returned from the morgue and had the doctor's report with him.

The inspector waved him through.

'This is for you...' said Gordon as he placed the folder on the table.

'Can you remind me of your name?'

'Gordon Craig, sir, in service at *Greystone* since 18 September of...'

'I just need the name, thank you.' The inspector interrupted him, hinting a smile as he looked at the report. 'Dr Henry Burlow...' he whispered to himself.

'He's the town doctor, sir...' suggested Gordon, '...but he's worked with the police for many years. He is a competent and very professional person.'

'I have no doubt about it, I will meet him in person tomorrow, but first I want to take a look at Inspector Morgan's office and residence. How many hotels or inns are there in the village besides the one I'm staying at?'

'Just one, Sir. *The Count's Inn* is on the right along Main Street, just past the old animal trough.'

'To begin with, go there and ask if there are any outsiders who have rented a room in the last two weeks. Also... Stop calling me sir... Inspector is more than enough,' he added in a more relaxed tone.

'All right, Inspector.' Gordon replied before he left the office.

After finishing the cigar, he inspected his colleague's office in detail. On his desk he kept some folders, divided between those containing closed cases and those with unsolved and still open cases. He checked them one by one but, among the many, the one concerning the book theft was missing. Thinking that Inspector Morgan could consider it so secondary that he did not consider it necessary to have an official file, he looked for scattered notes or sheets of paper, opening the drawers of the desk and those of a writing desk. Again, he found nothing useful.

– It's almost as if he wasn't working on this case. – He thought as he was going through the files and out of the office. He asked Jacob, who, however, not only confirmed that the entire police station had been put to work on finding the manuscript, but that Inspector Morgan seemed rather nervous in the last few days.

'Show me where his house is.'

'I must inform you that you will find the front door locked.'

'Don't worry about that.'

The sky had meanwhile become overcast and the pale morning sun had disappeared behind the grey clouds. It seemed like a setting day when it had just passed thirteen. A light sleet gave way to a more copious snowfall, with the roads slowly disappearing under the white blanket. Dorian Bayley wore a woolly hat, lifted his coat lapel and walked the streets of the village with his hands in his pockets. He had instructed Jacob Young to go to Vernon Doyle's house to take a look and to warn him if he found anything interesting.

Before leaving Main Street he noticed the inn sign on the right, with the ground floor used as a pub. The window panes were frosted and brightly coloured, while the front door was inlaid with a huge beer mug bent at forty-five degrees; a great place to get information about the habits of the inhabitants. He relaxed in the silence surrounding him, lulled by the muffled sound of footsteps in the snow and the condensed breath coming out of his mouth. He had already forgotten the endless journey that had led him to that remote corner of England and felt a strange feeling of familiarity with the environments he was beginning to know. If there wasn't a case to follow, he could really consider that stay as a reward holiday offered by his colleagues.

***

Nevil Morgan's cottage was isolated and fenced off with a low fence. All around it alternated country landscapes and wooded areas of evergreen trees. Beyond the main road, the inspector noticed a path starting from the south and disappearing into a grove, which stretched out towards the river. The fresh snow had now erased all traces. Like the others, this was a two-storey house with a sloping roof, built with dark bricks. Dorian Bayley stood in front of the door, pulled out a semi-rigid case and took two small tools as long as a finger of a hand and as thin as blades, beginning to play with the door patch. A few seconds later a click was heard; he put the tools back in order in the case, put it in his pocket and went inside, making sure no one had noticed him. He began to inspect the upper floor used as a study, a single room where everything seemed to be in order and carefully catalogued. Nevil Morgan used to duplicate the reports of the cases he followed, the folders were classified in chronological order and each contained: medical reports, interrogations, search results, a notebook for notes and personal considerations; the cover included the name of the case, the date of the beginning and end of the investigation, with the words "resolved" or "opened". He controlled them one by one until the most recent one, dating back to 18 September and relating to a fraud case, in which a Manchester investor had attempted to buy land in *Greystone,* using laundered money from illegal activities. The folder was classified as "Case Solved, 28 September 1884". He double-checked them by randomly opening them and reading the final report, but on the theft of the manuscript it seemed that Inspector Morgan had not opened any files or even kept a notebook. The house showed no signs of theft and the door had not been forced in any way. He opened the side drawers of the desk, then went to the central one, which was locked, picked up the case and pulled out a curved tool, put it in the lock, which gave up shortly afterwards. The interior was empty, he reflected for a moment and then closed it again, finished inspecting the floor and went down to the lower one. But even here the search was in vain; he was about to get up when he heard a noise coming from his left. He turned around and suspected that someone, spying on him from the window, had unintentionally bumped into the glass; he looked out but saw nothing.

'Maybe it's just an animal.'

However, he wanted to check and went out; he went around and went near the window on the outside of the house, the footprints printed on the snow left no doubt. Someone, after him, had walked to the door of the house without entering, then went to the window, but when Bayley had turned around after the noise, he had fled and disappeared into the woods. There was no point in trying to chase him; whoever it was had accumulated at least three minutes' lead, and once he reached the village the footprints would disappear. However, he thought it useful to evaluate his features and judged him to be a rather tall man wearing shoes or boots with non-slip soles.

Upon returning to Morgan's home, Dorian Bayley felt that something was wrong. He had been the only person to enter that house since the day of Nevil Morgan's disappearance, yet he felt that there was one important detail that was eluding him, something that was right in front of his eyes but only recorded with the least controllable part of his mind. It was like perceiving an object in the dark; he knew it was there, he could sense its texture but could not focus on its contours. He positioned himself with his back to the south wall of the room so that he could get a full view. He recorded the shape and arrangement of the furniture and windows, and finally noted his perplexity in the notebook. Immediately afterwards he went out, closed the door and walked towards Main Street. He wanted to go to the police station to get the doctor's report and talk to Gordon, then go back to the inn and arrange his luggage. He was counting on the fact that the material he had accumulated and the depositions he had collected would give him a lead. He usually ignored unsubstantiated theories, but he would have bet two shillings that there was a link between the theft of the manuscript and the disappearance of Nevil Morgan.

'Call Gordon and have him come to me,' the inspector told Jacob as he disappeared into his office.

'Right away, Inspector.'

Two minutes later he heard a knock and let the young policeman in.

'Did you find what I asked for?'

'Yes, Inspector!' He answered as he handed a small bag containing a small object.

'Where did you find it?'

'I searched the room since you told me what to look for. Finally, I found it under a desk, the first one to the left of the wall opposite the entrance.'

Dorian Bayley took the doctor's report and the object, wrote a note and said, 'Gordon good work.'

'I'll see you tomorrow and remember that information about the guests at the inns.'

'It will be done today.'

28 October 1750

A lukewarm wind crept through the branches of the tall oak trees, which lost their quietness and hissed out. From time to time, Sheriff Harvey would stop to look at the gnarled trunks of the older ones, tracing with his finger the contours of some engraved marks, and then resume his journey along a path covered with a thick layer of dry leaves. The sun struggled to penetrate the dense vegetation, leaving the forest in a perennial half-light hood, which had allowed an intricate undergrowth to create an almost uniform mantle. The villagers avoided it because they were convinced it was a place infested with restless spirits, who screamed their fury through the howls of wolves and the strange sounds of nocturnal animals.

After crossing a wooden bridge that cut through a stream, the sheriff continued to stay close to the shore, only to leave it and disappear into a path that cut through the thick vegetation and penetrated into its bowels. Some creepers descended from a steep rock face like thick twisted filaments, at a point where the undergrowth gave way to a damp, black soil to its extreme edge, where the trees stood as centuries-old guards of those silent places. After the clearing, he accelerated his pace, making his way with a stick; he wanted to reach his destination before nightfall. When in the distance he saw a small column of smoke rising towards the sky, he put on his hood and approached with caution, overcame the remains of a fence now collapsed, stopping just before an old shack used as a barn. Some pigs were locked up in an adjacent pigsty intent on grunting and sinking the black faces in the mud, a little further on a red haired cat was crouching on the edges of a well dug in the rock.

'Madame Althea,' he called in a low tone of voice.

There didn't seem to be a soul around, even though a column of grey smoke kept rising from the chimney.

'Madame Althea...' he repeated, taking a few steps towards the door and knocking discreetly, from the back of the house he heard a rapid ticking sound approaching. He went down the steps of the porch and saw a large dog that had stopped a few steps away from him, growling and staring at him in a threatening manner. When it was about to attack it changed its expression completely and knelt down; the woman knelt down to give it a quick caress.

'Follow me!' She said without stopping to look at him.

Her hair was long and white, frayed and disorderly, with an enigmatic face marked by time and toil. She walked bent but energetically and wore worn-out clothes that ended up fluttering around her ankles.

Entering the house she lit a candle and put it in the middle of the table, then revived the fire in the fireplace and placed a bundle of herbs hanging from a wall.

Sheriff Harvey took off the hood and stood on the edge of the door that was left open.

'I've written a letter that I've already delivered.'

Madame Althea turned and, for the first time, her dark and expressive eyes stared at those of the sheriff.

'The animals are restless, the branches of the trees beaten by a wind that comes from dark worlds. Soon powerful evil forces will leave the underworld to mingle among men.'

A reel lifted a bunch of leaves and the dog started playing with them trying to grab them. The sheriff remained silent watching Madame Althea, who in the meantime, had resumed her chores as if nothing had happened.

'The fiftieth night of Samhain is coming, the beast must be imprisoned and plunged into darkness.'

Sheriff Harvey moved to get her out and the woman returned to her animals ignoring his presence, he followed her to the edge of the pigsty.

'We'll wait for you in the place you know!' He said before he lifted the hood of the long robe he had worn to get there.

'It smells like death,' Madame Althea whispered cryptically as she disappeared into the back of the house followed by the big dog.

22 October 1884 – Wednesday

The crisp morning air would come in through the office window and sway the curtains. Dorian Bayley had got up early and walked the streets of the village just after breakfast. It was a useful exercise to put his ideas in order, taking advantage of the silence that still enveloped the village.
Sitting behind the desk, he left his mind free to wander in search of an intuition that could help him untangle the skeins that the case had put in front of him. He loved to mix the bitter aftertaste of the cigar with the sweet aftertaste of tea, a ritual he never escaped and which anticipated every day he worked.
'I've only been out of London two days and already I miss Emily's tea,' he thought with a grin and swallowed a sip.
After giving one last deep pull of the cigar, he held the smoke in his mouth and exhaled it without haste, looking the wood out the window; he heard a knock as he closed it.
'Come in!'
'Inspector, Dr Burlow has arrived and asks to speak with you,' announced Gordon Craig.
'Let him pass, and when you see him leave, come back to me.'
Henry Burlow was a distinguished man in his sixties, although his baldness and white beard made him appear later in life. He dressed with taste and his bearing betrayed a meticulous and calculated manner. Over his jacket he wore a short black cape. Before sitting down, he took off his top hat, opened his bag and took out some

documents that he gave to the inspector, then took some more and put on a pair of glasses.

'Thank you for showing up so early, Dr Burlow,' Dorian Bayley began as he started flipping through the files.

'In view of the state of the victim, I thought it appropriate to brief you as soon as possible. There is no doubt that this murder has special characteristics and that the case deserves the utmost caution. Let me add that I was shocked by the death of Vernon Doyle; I knew him very little, but everyone in the village spoke well of him.'

When he was in charge of an investigation, Dorian Bayley liked to limit conversations to the essentials, avoiding any digression that might lead him to stray from the nodal issues.

'I read from your preliminary report that Vernon Doyle bled to death from stab wounds and that the main one was inflicted on his carotid artery.'

'Exactly! The death occurred within a few tens of seconds; someone struck him in the throat with extreme ferocity, ripping his throat open almost to the point of decapitating him. Then he made two more cuts to the abdomen, which caused the bowels to spill.'

'Do you think this is the chronological sequence of the hits?'

'I think I can answer you with almost absolute certainty. The first blow was delivered to the neck, just below the jaw, and proved to be the fatal blow. From the angle and the laceration of the tissues, I was able to reconstruct the trajectory of the weapon, which goes from right to left. The killer showed an uncommon physical force, as he was able to use the cutting knife holding his wrist straight and his arm at ninety degrees to the body.'

'A left-handed man,' the inspector thought, 'unless...', his mind suggested but left the thought unanswered.

Dorian Bayley resumed reading the report, then looked up:
'What can you tell me about the other two wounds?'
'Same angle of the blows but delivered with less energy; enough, however, to open his abdomen and to reach the internal organs,' he replied without betraying the slightest emotion.
'Have you studied the wounds on the palm of the right hand?'
'Of course! These are shallow cuts, perhaps made by a small knife or a small sharp object, but certainly not by the murder weapon.'
'How can you be sure?'
'The width of the cuts is minimal, while the blade used to kill will have been at least half an inch thick.'
'A big hunting knife?'
'Possible!'
'What time can death be traced?'
'I examined the body around eleven o'clock; considering the temperature in the church and the muscular rigidity of the corpse, I would say that death occurred between three and five in the morning.'
The medical-scientific preparation that Dr Burlow demonstrated and the way in which he was able to explain it with natural simplicity, showed his deep acuity. After reading a medical report, Dorian Bayley used to study the body of a victim himself, to make sure that the work done was meticulous; he thought that in that circumstance there would be no need.
'I read from your personal notes that you also specialize in criminal psychology. So, Dr Burlow, I ask you only in confidence: what criminal mind can come to rage in such a brutal way on a body after the victim is already dead?'

'I assume you're referring to the two abdominal wounds. I would say that this is a man with a deviant mind, what in criminal medicine is defined as a psychopath, without any inhibitory brake and able to deny any value to the life of others. Without a doubt, we are dealing with an individual of male sex, vigorous, with chronic sexual dysfunction, probably distracted by the desire to achieve a mission that only he knows.'

'Why are you talking about a mission?'

'In the past, I've studied several cases of insane individuals responsible for murder. Sometimes there was no apparent motive and immediately afterwards, the murderer tended to close in on himself, in a sort of post-traumatic vegetative state, becoming a subject no longer dangerous to the community. Other times, instead, the motive was to be sought in some form of mystical conviction, a sort of superior design, in which inner voices coming from who knows where ordered him to eliminate victims considered impure or blasphemous for some reason. I classified these cases among the most dangerous because the subjects in question consider the first murder as the beginning of an initiatory path which, in order to be carried out, foresees several others.'

'Are you talking about a religious sect?'

Dr Burlow stared at the inspector as he took off his glasses.

'It can be a sect like an anarchist group, or a revolutionary army. In life, Inspector, there are and always will be leaders and followers. You only have to convince a follower that you're pursuing a higher purpose and there will be few things you won't do to achieve it.'

'Have you ever heard of religious sects operating in *Greystone*?' He asked Dorian Bayley directly.

'In this village two mentalities coexist; superstition and magical religious beliefs are flanked by the concreteness of daily life, demonstrating the vitality typical of a place that resides isolated, far from the big cities. In *Greystone* centuries-old traditions survive and the inhabitants maintain a relationship with nature that has little to do with the laws of science. If you want to solve the case, you cannot ignore the phenomenon.'

'Thank you for your time, Dr Burlow. You've been very thorough,' the inspector concluded after a few moments of reflection.

'Duty!' The doctor replied laconically as he put on his cape and walked towards the door with the cylinder in his hand. Before leaving, however, he turned towards the inspector.

'I almost forgot; Father Beathan asked me when the body could be released. He would like to celebrate the funeral tomorrow.'

'If it's all right with you, Dr Burlow, let's get on with it.'

Not even two minutes later, Gordon Craig appeared.

'Do you have that information I asked you yesterday?'

The young officer opened his notepad, but he only spoke by giving it a little peek once in a while.

'As for the *Count's Inn,* only two guests have stayed in the last fortnight: a London insurance agent, Anthony White, who left *Greystone* on the morning of 21 October. The man was in the village on a matter of buying and selling some land disputed by two families. During his stay, he was a guest on the estate inside the stables of Peter Penninghton, with whom he rode out on horseback on the morning of 20 October, together with three other witnesses. They all confirmed that they spent the evening together and retired very late, not before four o'clock.

The other client is Father Graves, who spends short periods in the village to soothe the effects of a lung

disease he has suffered from in recent years. But I inform you that the priest also has an alibi.'
'What's that?'
'Age!' The agent replied, 'Father Graves is almost 90 years old and only God knows how he is still standing.'
'...what about the inn where I'm staying?'
'There's something interesting in the inn where you live. A stranger arrived in *Greystone* on the morning of 13 October. He booked until the 26th but the owner has not seen him since yesterday, when he left for the last time around eleven.'
'Another mysterious disappearance?' Dorian Bayley asked concerned.
'I'd say no. His name is Darrel Bennet and he's an art dealer from Manchester. The man had never been seen in the village until that day. When he left he took everything he had with him, so his removal is to be considered voluntary. He paid in advance for his entire stay and left without leaving messages and without asking for his money back for the days when he did not sleep in the inn.'
'Darrel Bennet...' whispered Dorian Bayley in a low voice to fix the name in his mind. 'A check must be carried out by our colleagues in London. A man who appears out of nowhere on the day the book is stolen, and disappears on the day of the murder is, to say the least, suspicious. Telegraph all the information you have at Scotland Yard, ask as a matter of urgency for detailed information about him and in the meantime ask around if anyone has seen him in the pubs, in the main streets, but above all question railway station employees.'

23 October 1884 – Thursday

As he crossed the Ducks Bridge, Dorian Bayley was busy rummaging through his thoughts in a vain attempt to give substance to the strange sensation felt the previous day in Nevil Morgan's house. Subsequent events had overshadowed that sense of disorientation that now deserved to be analysed carefully, exploiting the complicity of the fresh air that *Greystone* generously gave out in the morning. He crossed the bridge and continued on to the road to St. Patrick's Square, the place where Vernon Doyle's body was found. He walked around the church and continued for a stretch until he came across the property of Judge Frank Owen, surrounded by a wooden fence and tall, broad-stemmed trees. He stood open-mouthed to observe its dimensions; one could not see its entire perimeter as it was so vast. The interior of the estate included a huge two-storey villa, an elegant garden, a small building used as an annexe and, what struck him the most, an expanse of woodland that was lost in width and depth, giving the context a picturesque quiet.

The wrought iron gate that opened in the garden was closed, but as soon as the inspector rattled the bell hanging from the upper stanchion, a young woman met him on her way out the front door.

'You must be Inspector Dorian Bayley, officer Young came by last night to announce your visit; my name is Margaret and I am the judge's housekeeper', she began with a gentle smile as she yanked the moving part of the gate towards her.

The inspector bowed his head in greeting.

'Nice to meet you Margaret, can Judge Owen see me?'

'Please, Inspector, follow me, I'll show you the way.'

Dorian Bayley was seated in a huge room that served both as an atrium and reception area and waited seated next to a large, sturdy beech wood table. An imposing fireplace had just been lit and the heat it gave off was not enough to warm the whole room. The inspector looked around with interest. The judge had been the last person to see Nevil Morgan before he disappeared into thin air and could at best be an absolutely reliable witness. On the walls a series of paintings depicting men of the past in robes and headgear that, it was legitimate to believe, represented the lineage from which he came.

A powerful voice made Dorian Bayley jump, and he turned round suddenly.

'At last I have the honour to make your acquaintance Inspector Bayley,' announced Frank Owen with a tenor tone, whose impetuousness had an artificial appearance.

'I'm the one to be honoured, Judge Owen, and I apologise if I've been such an early bird to visit you, but Vernon Doyle's funeral is at nine o'clock and I imagine we'll all be at the ceremony.'

'The early hours of the morning are perfect for conversation, Inspector, also because I suspect that you have your urgencies and I have my duties.'

Having said that, he called Margaret and threw a red ribbon down from a support hanging next to a window.

'Can I help you, Your Honour?' the woman asked after she entered.

'Margaret, please serve two hot teacups with a tray of butter biscuits. Then get my dress ready for the funeral, make it presentable this time.'

'It will be done!' Margaret answered before leaving the room.
'Tell me, how does our beautiful country look, Inspector?'
'It seems pervaded by a fascinating aura; the stone houses, the surrounding woods, the stream with the ancient bridge, the hills that can be seen from the window of my lodging, is like a fairy tale landscape.'
'And I assure you it is! Although, as you well know, unfortunately these days strange things are happening.'
Margaret returned to the room with a tray on which she had elegantly placed some homemade biscuits of various shapes, a crockery sugar bowl, a steaming teapot and two teacups.
'No, Margaret!' The judge scolded her irritated, 'These are not the cups we use when there are important guests!
Dorian Bayley would have said they were going more than fine, but Margaret was already taking them away to replace them; in a matter of moments she was again holding those "for important guests", made of silver, with a wide handle and a relief depicting a coat of arms, to which the inspector did not recognise any significance.
'Now, over a good breakfast, please ask me anything you can think of to help you get to grips with the absurd incidents that are taking place in the village and that have shaken the inhabitants up quite a bit,' said the satisfied judge.
'From the report I read you were the last person to see Inspector Nevil Morgan on the morning of 18 October,' began the Inspector from Scotland Yard by pulling out his notebook.
'I think so, he dropped by around 8:00, as is often the case when he has some free time and has been entertained for about 20 minutes. We are friends and

often talk about things that have nothing to do with our work.'

'And did he tell you where he was going once he got out of here?'

'No, but I think he was going to the office. Before he disappeared, he was investigating the theft of an ancient manuscript in the home of Adam Ford, the cemetery caretaker.'

The judge took a break, had a sip of tea and then resumed.

'You know, Inspector, in these parts a theft doesn't happen every day, so even what may seem to you a small crime for which it's not worth your soul, here deserves deep attention, and it's on this dimension that Nevil Morgan was moving.'

'To your knowledge, was it a valuable book?'

'I don't know. Inspector Morgan had confided in me that it was an esoteric manuscript, which contained ancient magic formulas useful for obtaining the favours of some supernatural force. He didn't add much else. Nevil Morgan is a man of integrity in his profession and is not in the habit of blabbing for the country about matters concerning ongoing investigations, even if it were simply theft of a cigar.'

'Before his disappearance, did Nevil Morgan seem strange, nervous? Was he afraid of something or someone?'

Judge Owen put a cookie in his mouth and chewed it and tasted its sweet taste. He accompanied it with another sip of tea and started talking again, with the usual amplified tone.

He placed two fingers under his chin to reflect better. 'I didn't notice anything, his behaviour seemed to me like always. He didn't show any of this or at least nothing that showed any concern.'

Frank Owen pulled a silver watch out of his vest pocket to check the time. The inspector realised the judge was eager to begin preparations for the funeral.
'Just two more questions.'
Frank Owen nodded.
'Did you know Vernon Doyle?'
'I knew him by sight and we would wave at each other whenever we met, but other than that, I never had any kind of relationship with him. On the other hand, I am not a frequent visitor to the church, let alone to the inns in the village. My position demands a rather strict protocol.'
'Have you seen any strangers hanging around the village recently?'
'I'm sorry I can't be of any help to you on this either...' he spread his arms in despair, '...but I didn't see anyone except the *Greystone* people.'
Thoughtful, Dorian Bayley closed the notebook and thanked the judge, who ordered Margaret to accompany the inspector to the gate.
'See you at the funeral,' she said before she took her leave of him.
If he'd hoped to get useful information from that conversation, Dorian Bayley was forced to agree that he'd blown a gasket. That tall, sturdy man, with a loud voice and a prominent belly, had revealed nothing to him that could help him unravel a few skeins. But perhaps, he thought, he could still get something out of that visit.
When Margaret opened the gate, Bayley stepped out but immediately turned around.
'Can you tell me Margaret, if it is your custom to accompany every guest who leaves the judge's house?' He asked in confidence.
'I always do it inspector, by express will of the master.'

Despite her work clothes, Margaret expressed a youthful charm sweetened by a calm way of speaking and a mild and pleasant tone of voice, in perfect contrast to that of the judge. Her hair was gathered in a white cotton cap, with light brown curls sprouting out of it, and her slender body hidden by a long dress that went down to her ankles; Dorian Bayley couldn't attribute an age to her, but he thought it difficult for her to be over thirty.

'That goes for close friends like Nevil Morgan, too, right?'

'That's right, Nevil Morgan is a frequent visitor to the house but I always personally escort him out.'

'Can you tell me if the last day he left this house he was on his way to his office?'

'We didn't talk at all but... Thinking about it...' a ray of sunshine lit up Margaret's smile '...he had the bag with him.'

'So?' Asked Bayley intrigued.

'Inspector Morgan is a very methodical man; he only brings his records with him when he has to make inquiries. I'm sure he wasn't on his way to the office.'

When the villa gate closed, Dorian Bayley paused to finish his notes. At the bottom of the page, in bad handwriting, he had written:

'Judge Owen doesn't seem upset about the disappearance of his friend / reticent, maybe he's lying / hiding something?

***

Before dissolving the funeral celebration and starting the burial, Father Beathan wanted to honour the deceased with a speech that he had pinned down for the occasion on some sheets of paper bound and placed on the desk.

'Every event, even the most terrible, hides a divine project, so immense and articulated, that it is for us, humble mortals, incomprehensible. The relief of an ultimate goal, sublime and right, cannot and must not mitigate that feeling of compassion and that feeling of lacerating pain that an entire community, gathered here, feels towards the victim of such brutality.'

While with his right hand he pointed out the numerous countrymen present, giving blessings, with the other hand he turned the page and continued.

'A man who has served his church for decades, with honesty, dedication and immense love. A man who chose to be alone, as the sun, in history, were the closest creatures to God. Vernon Doyle was the symbol of that humble, helpful, devoted person that we all aspire to be. An example of virtue concealed in a solitary, introverted character, but capable of generous impulses and self-sacrifice so pure that he considered himself the closest virtue to God.'

Even the wind seemed to have died down to hear Father Beathan's speech. The words were spoken in a solemn, almost unreal silence, and every single sentence came straight into the consciences of those present just as any speech Father Beathan professed with his heart, capable as he was, of drawing attention and awakening feelings dormant in the depths of the soul.

During the celebration Dorian Bayley had done nothing but look around discreetly, looking for looks, signs of nervousness, interactions between the participants and any other behaviour that might reveal signs of possible relations between the inhabitants, and between them and the late Vernon Doyle. Every now and then, pretending to stretch his legs, he would walk along the space where the participants were crowded, observing their faces and their movements. He recognized the blacksmith George Davies with his showy beard and the judge Frank Owen, with whom he had exchanged a nod of greeting. There were both of his collaborators, Jacob Young and Gordon Craig, who he had instructed to keep their eyes open if they noticed anything strange. A third officer on duty at *Greystone* had been forced to leave the country to visit his sick mother after a letter from Nottingham informed him of her deteriorating health. Before Father Beathan delivered his final speech, Dorian Bayley had approached Gordon Craig, who had pointed out to him a couple who were attending the funeral together with a boy in his twenties.

'That's Adam Ford, the graveyard keeper, along with his wife Olivia and his son Martin, just back from Liverpool, where he lives and works. He is the one who reported the book stolen,' he told the inspector as he put his ear to his mouth to listen better.

'I'll go talk to him after the service, go warn him and ask him to wait for me in the house. What about that man next to Judge Owen?' He asked looking the other way.

The officer took a sneak peek under the pretence of fixing his helmet.

'Mayor Montgomery Chapman. An honest man of few words.'

When the celebration came to an end, those present went to the cemetery gate to earn their way out and Inspector Bayley found himself in the middle of a small crowd. Just a few steps away was George Davies who, meanwhile, had approached an acquaintance.

'I'll be at the Golden Pub after dinner,' he was saying to the man.

Dorian Bayley stared at what he had just heard, intent on taking the opportunity to question him again.

***

The killing of Vernon Doyle seemed to have exposed sensitive nerves in the community. On the faces of those present at the funeral, Dorian Bayley could read a sadness and sincere emotion. There was something else in the air, however, but the inspector was able to give him a name only once he entered the driveway that led to Adam Ford's home; it was fear. He had seen it in the eyes of many during Father Beathan's oration, in the disorientated looks of the women who watched in silence and in the expressions of Mr and Mrs Ford, their son and even the officers who collaborated in the investigation.

He clearly understood that, in a small and seemingly united community, the occurrence of heinous crimes and unmotivated disappearances represented unexpected traumas and that it took time to forget, look beyond and feel safe again. It was clear that the capture of the culprits would reassure the inhabitants of *Greystone*, giving them a chance to speed up the process of removal and return to their usual lives.

The sun illuminating the bright blue sky was a welcome surprise, which Dorian Bayley welcomed with pleasure. He thought it was time to shed some light on some of the elements concerning the beginning of the whole thing, starting from the Ford's house, where everything had started with the theft of the book. The more time went by, the more indissoluble became the belief that all the events that followed were linked together. In his heart, he feared that a new link would soon be added to that chain of mystery and violence.

He exhaled the last cloud of smoke from his mouth, put out his cigar and slipped it into a tin container, which he slipped into his left pocket. In the opposite pocket he looked for the notebook, but he found between his fingers a piece of paper folded into four parts. He took it out and saw that the handwriting was unknown to him. He unfolded the note and read it. It was a small list of names marked with Roman numerals:

I - Invocation
II - Appearance
III - Imprisonment
IV - Expulsion to the underworld

There was nothing else written on it and there was no signature.

'When I left the cemetery taking advantage of the gathering, someone must have slipped it into my pocket,' he thought intrigued.

He had a quick think to remember a face or figure wandering suspiciously around the moment the small crowd had been at the exit gate, but in vain. He might as well have focused on what they were trying to tell him and why; perhaps only then he would have traced the identity of the author of the ticket.

He decided not to think about it for the moment; after a few steps, he found himself in front of Adam Ford's house. He knocked and stretched his ear inwards, but he heard nothing. Gordon Craig, during Doyle's burial, had gone to warn Adam Ford that he would be home within an hour, and he said there would be no problem. He knocked louder, but again he got no answer. He walked around the house, a rather modest building surrounded by a small garden full of loose work items and weeds that were growing wild without anybody to prune them. He peered through the windows, but inside, he didn't see anyone. He opened a window left ajar at the back, realizing that the locking system was broken, and from there, he began to hear muffled voices coming from upstairs, where it seemed as if someone was arguing in a heated discussion. These were male voices interspersed, from time to time, by a woman who seemed intent on softening the tone of the discussion. From downstairs she could only distinguish a few single pieces, such as 'it's not the case,' 'silence,' 'I couldn't.' Then he distinctly heard the sound of a door opening; the voices became clearer, but the discussion had now ended. So, as not to be discovered, he went to the front door again and knocked as if he had just arrived. A few seconds later Adam Ford opened the door and let him in. He was a short, thin man, with an incipient baldness, an unshaven beard, dark eyes hollowed in his eye sockets and raven hair that gave him a gloomy appearance. Sitting around the table were his son Martin and his wife who, upon being introduced, stood up and bowed.

'Do you have any suspicions about who might be interested in breaking into your house and stealing that book without touching anything else?' Dorian Bayley asked.

'No!' Adam Ford replied. 'I don't suspect anyone! Anyone could have broken in and stolen anything else. At the back of the house, one of the windows lost its support and could be opened with a simple push. I've been calling George Davies for days to have it repaired.'

Adam Ford tried to simulate a relaxed attitude but, from the look of his eyes, he betrayed a nervousness and moved in jerks.

'Why steal a worthless book?' Dorian Bayley insisted.

'You shouldn't ask me, Inspector; there are many lovers of esotericism and magic in the village. Maybe he was a collector, an amateur or something, someone who mistakenly believed he could make a profit.'

Dorian Bayley doubted what Adam Ford was telling him. He looked into his son Martin's eyes. The inspector knew he was outside *Greystone* the night of the robbery, but he wanted to find out if he knew anything after he arrived. However, the young man seemed to say with a look, 'I know nothing about it.'

His wife Olivia, on the other hand, kept her face bent down and her hands closed on her knees. She merely nodded to confirm whatever her husband said. She then decided, without too many words, to get to the heart of the matter.

'Mr Ford, where were you between 3:00 and 5:00 a.m. Thursday morning, 21 October?'

'I was asleep, like every night! I never get up before six.' he replied, without getting upset.

The wife nodded her head, like she was trained to confirm everything.

The inspector noted the statement before slipping the conversation about Nevil Morgan; here, too, however, he did not get any useful information.

'It's hard to believe an experienced inspector like Nevil Morgan would disappear because a worthless manuscript was stolen. But what if that book was priceless and it was Vernon Doyle who stole it and the inspector, before he disappeared, came to you, Mr Ford, and confided his suspicions in him? You would have had a motive to get revenge on the librarian with whom, I'm guessing, you had other unfinished business. You'd have been a suspect in the eyes of Nevil Morgan and therefore, before you killed Doyle...'

'You're delirious!!!' Screamed Adam Ford. 'This is absurd! Nevil Morgan had been my friend for years and I had no reason to hurt Vernon Doyle, whom I barely knew.'

'Calm down, I'm just putting the facts together,' he said calmly.

'Facts? What facts? That I would kill two people to retrieve an old book?'

Dorian Bayley stared at Adam Ford's gaze; in fact he knew that he was drawing conclusions without any concrete clue, but intuition suggested that the cemetery keeper was hiding something from him and that, by intimidating him, he might be able to dig a few spiders out of the hole.

'Thank you for your availability,' he concluded laconically as he closed the notebook. 'I'll need to speak to you in the next few days as well.'

'Whatever. I have nothing to hide. You can find me at the cemetery or here in the house.'

A suspicious silence fell in the room.

Leaving the house, the inspector took with him the belief that every person questioned was hiding a secret. The problem was to understand whether what was being hidden from him was about the disappearance of Nevil Morgan and the murder of Vernon Doyle, or whether it was a secret that had settled in personal and collective history that, out of distrust or a sense of belonging, was not revealed even in the face of events of unprecedented gravity such as those that had recently occurred.

Adam Ford waited for the inspector to leave; from a locked cupboard he took a hunting knife, then put on his coat, hat and ran out. He was sure that, if he hadn't done something, with a guy like Dorian Bayley certain secrets wouldn't last long.

***

A pile of grey clouds began to cover the sky. The days had shortened but, in spite of this, in the early hours of the afternoon, immediately after lunch, all activities seemed to cease in the village; in those moments one could enjoy a silence that Dorian Bayley could not remember ever having heard even in the quietest parts of London.

He'd been in the office all morning sorting through his notes and ideas. He had preferred not to inform his agents about the note he had received; being accustomed to never dismissing any hypothesis in advance, there was a remote possibility that one of them had slipped it into his pocket.

Back at the inn on Kings Street, he rinsed up and shaved. Then he used some brandy and sat down on the small table in his room, opening the curtains in the window. He began to look up at the sky and the forest, which, perched on the hill, stood further away. He had just finished writing to his wife, exalting the beauty and charm of that remote place, where everything seemed to flow with different ways and times than the reality where he had been living and working for years. For lunch the innkeeper had served him an abundant potato stew, vegetables seasoned with local spices and roasted chestnuts. He felt full and sleepy and thought it was better to lie down on the bed and rest, before returning to the police station and see if there was anything new. When he opened his eyes again, the sky was already near sunset. Unaware of the wind that had risen and the darker and darker clouds that threatened rain, he took a walk through the village. He arrived at St. Patrick's Square, where a group of boys were talking and giggling. He recognized Martin Ford, Adam's son, intent on telling the experiences of Liverpool to his old friends. Instead of turning left and taking Main Street, Dorian Bayley decided to take a right along a path that wedged into the woods. After a few minutes' walk the vegetation opened up, leaving room for a green and well-tended lawn. Almost out of nowhere, a little house with a fenced garden and a sloping roof appeared; it was Father Beathan's home. The gate, as was customary there, was open, and Dorian Bayley tried in vain to knock; at that hour, he thought, the priest was in church. He continued his walk, wedging himself into the woods, along a narrow path that crossed the main one and led eastward, towards Judge Owen's villa. He met the river which, at that point, was reduced to a sort of stream, because of a layer of stones that had been laid on its bed to allow the animals to cross. Dorian Bayley crossed it along the same path. Darkness was now imminent. He decided to speed up the pace and, after a while, appeared near a farm. To his right were large flat pastures with sheep, cows and horses still grazing. He turned around the farm, passing to the left and skirting the river again in the direction of the village centre. Further ahead you could catch a glimpse of the church and, further to the right, even further away, the judge's house.

'Don't do it, for God's sake, don't do it!'

A shrill female voice forced him to turn around; an old lady, with her head covered in a colourful veil and wearing a long peasant dress, approached him, stopping no more than five steps away.

'What did you say, excuse me?' Dorian Bayley asked, amazed.

He noticed that the lady was very skinny, with her face carved out by wrinkles and age, but still seemed energetic. She was holding a lamb in her arms, careless of its attempts to free itself from her grip.

'Run while you can, go back where you came from, don't stay any longer.'

The woman's tone was pleading and, in her lively gaze, there was a note of despair.

'Why should I leave *Greystone*?'
The inspector suspected that age was playing a nasty trick on the poor woman.
'Because nothing here is as it seems and we're all in danger. So are you.'
'Me too?' He echoed her.
'Look around. Don't you notice anything strange? Does it seem normal to you? It's just appearance.'
The peasant woman was pointing to the woods behind her and everything around them.
Dorian Bayley indulged her for not being rude, a defect he had always hated.
The little light that filtered made the branches of the trees shine a reddish colour in unison, lashed by sudden gusts of icy wind. All around, the darkness began to swallow the hills, while the first lights of the oil lamps flickered in the distance towards the centre of the village.
'I'm sorry, ma'am, but I don't notice anything.' He said quietly, shrugging his shoulders.
A few drops of water fell on the face of Dorian Bayley, who took the opportunity to wave goodbye in haste towards the Ducks Bridge.
'You'll get wet, Inspector...' cried the lady, '...come in the house and I'll show you something very interesting...'
Without stopping the pass Dorian Bayley turned his face backwards.
'I can't right now; good evening, madam.'
The peasant woman stood still shouting something incomprehensible, not caring about the rain that was beginning to increase in intensity.

***

As soon as the dinner, which he had decided to bring forward, Inspector Bayley crossed St Patrick Square again and then entered the alleyway where the Golden Pub, the evening gathering for many *Greystone*residents, *was* located. The rain had stopped and the damp air formed small banks of fog, which stratified into strange shapes, illuminated by the street lamps scattered along the streets of the village.

It was still early; the only four patrons present sat at a small table at the end of a long, narrow room with wooden tables, all of the same size, lined up on both sides. At the end of the room, on the left, there was a small door leading to the staff area, while on the wall, dull red in colour, there was a target with five darts and some small pictures representing the enchanting views of *Greystone*. Along the sidewalls, two lighted fireplaces welcomed the guests with the blessing of heat, refreshed them from the humidity and cold.

You could smell wine and wood and, intermittently, the aroma of the cigar that two of the four men sitting there were smoking. Dorian Bayley did the same while sitting on a bench in front of a table in the middle of the room, from where he could control the entrance to the place. He took the note out of his pocket and carefully reread its contents, trying to reflect on its meaning.

– Invocation, apparition, imprisonment, banishment to the underworld –

Those words didn't tell him anything but they had to hide an important and, above all, secret message if the author had taken care to keep his anonymity. The cryptic behaviour of many people said a lot about the complexity of the case and the relationship between the inhabitants of *Greystone*. He was reminded of the words of the woman he met near the farm and found himself laughing at himself at the mere thought of having given her a minimum of reliability. He asked the waitress to come back as soon as a friend who was waiting had arrived. In the meantime, he reread his notes for the umpteenth time, adding signs to them that went to join phrases apparently unrelated to each other.

Shortly afterwards, George Davies entered, preceded by a couple made up of an older gentleman with white hair and a younger man, who looked like his son. The inspector recalled seeing them both at the funeral. The blacksmith looked around to take his place but Dorian Bayley, raising his hand to hold the cigar, attracted his attention and invited him to come closer.

'I'd love to buy you a drink,' he proposed, widening his mouth into a big smile.

The iron craftsman smiled for the first time, accepting the invitation willingly. They called the waitress and ordered two pints of a special local beer, brewed in the workshop of Tom Porter, a renowned master brewer who had been producing and exporting it for over a century throughout the country.

The inspector told about his life in London, its rhythms, the many events that followed and that made it a lively, industrious and protracted city but, at the same time, complicated and violent. When the subject moved on to the life of George Davies and the inhabitants of *Greystone*, the third mug of beer lay empty upside down on the table.

'Two more pints!' The blacksmith clamoured lifting it up and make it vibrate in the air.

The pub was three-quarters full and the patrons were mostly unknown to the inspector. George Davies, on the contrary, exchanged a nod of greeting with anyone who appeared in the room; he had finally disbanded and no longer looked like the man of few words Dorian Bayley had known on the day of the murder. He took the opportunity to change the subject.

'How well do you know Inspector Morgan?'

'Nevil Morgan is a respected character around here,' he began to tell the story on a freewheeling basis. Although essential and contaminated by a strong local accent, his dialectic was pleasant.

'He's everybody's friend; it often happens that he buys me a beer here at the Golden Pub, or that we meet in the village and exchange a few jokes, which I know of, about the weather, an event or something like that.'

'And did he ever say anything to you about the robbery at Adam Ford's house?'

'Adam Ford,' repeated the blacksmith with a mocking smile. 'That's a really weird guy, inspector. Hanging around the cemetery too much must have done him no good. His son Martin worked for me as an apprentice when he was 14, but even then, he dreamed of leaving *Greystone*. A few years later, in fact, he sneaked off to Liverpool and did it right. Have you visited the Ford house yet? Looks like a haunted place.' He said, bursting out with a thunderous laugh.

'We were saying...' Dorian Bayley tried to resume the conversation. '...if Inspector Morgan ever told you about the book theft.'

'Oh, excuse me, Inspector, but when I drink sometimes I let myself go. It's not my fault, it's that bloody Tom Porter. He makes an excellent beer and I can't resist it.' he added as he inaugurated a new mug.

After a generous sip, with foam on his moustache, he tried to pick up the thread.

'That's an ongoing investigation and Inspector Morgan doesn't like to talk about his cases until he's solved them...or at least not with us.'

'Who then?' He pressed the inspector.
'Eleanor. Madame Eleanor. Sometimes she helps the inspector with the investigation.'
'How?'
'Ha-ha-ha.' the blacksmith laughed with even more vigour bending his head backwards 'magic, séances, things like that. Do you understand, Inspector? Nevil Morgan spends his days visiting his friends because he knows that those few cases he gets his hands on are solved by Madame Eleanor. Or so they say in the village.'
'And do you think it's true?' Dorian Bayley asked, avoiding to take out the notebook to keep the conversation on a friendly level and not give the impression of being in an official capacity.
'Inspector, I am a blacksmith; for me all magic is locked inside a lock until I blow it up...' he chuckled again, '...and then I realize that nothing magical or mysterious is hidden behind it. But that's not the case in the village. Sometimes things seem to go differently. Maybe I'm missing something or maybe I'm not missing anything, it's just that I'm a little tipsy. As for Nevil Morgan, I can tell you he's a very good police inspector, who knows his job very well. He's got his own particular side, but then again, who doesn't?'
'This Madame Eleanor, do you know her?'
'I happened to see her a few times. She's a harmless old lady, but she looks like a poor fool. Unfortunately, many people don't think so. I know for a fact that Inspector Morgan is not alone in asking for her help. There are those who want to invoke the soul of some dear departed and those who want to know if something bad will happen to him and his family soon...'
'You don't believe in such things, do you?'

'As I told you before, I'm a practical guy. Are you familiar with the story circulating in the town about the discovery of Sarah Benson about 15 years ago?'

Dorian Bayley nodded no with his head. He was curious about how reality was perceived in *Greystone*, how it was filtered through credulity and superstition. In fact, before leaving London, he had carefully studied all of Inspector Morgan's cases, including that of little Sarah.

After finishing the umpteenth pint and asking the waitress to bring another, George Davies resumed.

'At the time the girl was five years old; she was the daughter of a couple of craftsmen who live around here. One evening she was lost in the woods. She later told that she was following in the footsteps of a strange animal never seen before, an animal so powerful and heavy that it left footprints three times wider and deeper than those of a bear.'

Seeing the waitress approaching, the blacksmith took a break. Before the girl could place the tray on the table, George Davies grabbed the mug and took a sip, pouring the beer over the sides of her face, while with his free hand he patted her bottom. Laughter of approval rose from the tables nearby.

'And how did it end?' The inspector pressed to bring him to order.

The blacksmith recomposed himself as best he could.

'She was found by Edward Lambert, a policeman on duty at *Greystone* who is now out for personal reasons. According to the version circulating in the village, the police officers were led by Nevil Morgan, who had relied on the information provided by Madame Eleanor during a séance he had attended with the girl's parents. I think they're out of their bloody minds! That little girl had run away like so many children run away when their parents are too busy thinking about themselves. What big monstrous animal could have been chasing after five years old? The fantasies of children and the delusions of a sorceress should remain where they are and instead here in the village of such stories circulate by the dozens, fantasies created by who knows what bizarre mind that, for many, become truths to fear.'

Dorian Bayley's mug was half full. He wanted to remain lucid to put together all the pieces of what George Davies was telling him while he was drunk.

'Now, if you don't mind, I have to go to the bathroom, if you'll excuse me...' said the blacksmith, taking a bow.

The inspector, left alone, hurried to get out his notebook. He had met Nevil Morgan many years earlier, hearing him speak many times about esoteric practices and higher, ethereal, otherworldly entities, all capable of changing the course of events and predicting the future. This made him consider the blacksmith's words reliable. He put aside his notebook and began to reflect. His gaze was lost in an unspecified spot in the smoke-filled hall.

'A propitiatory ritual for hunting...' he thought, '...many people welcome the hunting season with propitiatory rites of different kinds. At the base of these rites there is a symbology that can be found in some popular beliefs or in legends that are renewed over the centuries.'

He thought back to the story of the little girl who followed in the footsteps of a large animal and interpreted it as one of the symbols linked to the hunting ritual.

'The animal is first invoked, then sighted, captured and finally killed.'

It remained to be understood what this had to do with killing Vernon Doyle.

24 October 1884 – Friday

The words of the coroner, and the more confused words of George Davies, had made Inspector Dorian Bayley reflect, and began to find confirmation in the behaviour of the inhabitants. A village where superstition and spiritualism survived with such vigour could have reacted to Vernon Doyle's murder in an unpredictable way. The ramblings of the old peasant woman only confirmed that violence and fear could take the reins of a mind made orphaned of free, analytical and rational thought. Although convinced of the emptiness of a thought contaminated by superstition, he decided that the best behaviour was to adapt to the circumstances and individuals with whom he was confronted. The dark mentality that burdened the village, like a poisonous fog originating from the dark centuries of the past, greatly broadened the range of possible perpetrators of the murder.

'Convince a little man who's serving a higher cause and there will be few things he won't be willing to do.'

Who owned the hand that had gripped Vernon Doyle's body with inhuman ferocity? And more importantly, what or who pushed it?

Though unsupported by any evidence or findings, Dorian Bayley was beginning to flash in Dorian Bayley's head the idea that the murderer might not have acted on his own, but that it might be a crime that was part of a larger plan.

If there really were secret sects at *Greystone* and there were mediums or spiritual fathers who had some kind of religious mysticism, anyone could have lost their mind and made such a crazy gesture. It was necessary, therefore, to find out what secrets that apparently mild and tranquil village was hiding, if there really were evil forces operating underground and out of control. Dorian Bayley had grown up in a very religious family, but his legal and philosophical studies, his encounters with men of science and the horror of terrible crimes with which he had been living for almost thirty years of investigation, had convinced him of how the human being was the only monster to fear and how easy it became to read the mind of a criminal once unnecessary ideological trappings and surreal abstract beliefs had been eliminated.

As he crossed the old wooden bridge, he looked around to find the path that agent Jacob had advised him to cut through the main street and reach Mrs Eleanor's house as soon as possible. As soon as he was about to walk along it, inside a bush, he noticed that threatening shoals of low clouds were approaching the village. He lifted his coat lapel and accelerated his pace. Inside the vegetation, the pale sun gave way to a semi-shade broken here and there by rays of light breaking perpendicularly on the ground. From the mouth the breath began to come out condensing into small white clouds.

If it is true that Mrs Eleanor was considered by the inhabitants as a kind of healing medium and that she had established a deep relationship of trust with Nevil Morgan, knowing her and talking to her could have helped Dorian Bayley to acquire useful information, to try, at least, to draw up a psychological profile of her. Although the disappearance had no apparent motivation, the fact that both the theft and the murder had something to do with religion and the supernatural began to weave a thin thread that could connect the events.

When he came to the edge of the property, he was disappointed. He expected an elegant neoclassical style house, with statues, a garden and a well-kept driveway bordered by lush flowerbeds. He found in front of him a torn gate leaning crookedly on the fence that once supported the uprights, chickens flying everywhere and an improvised fence, where fat pigs basked in the mud. When he knocked, the door opened inwards, as the lock hook was without a padlock.

'Anybody here?'

A woman came down a crumbling staircase and sat him down. Her appearance perfectly matched the place where she lived. Mrs Eleanor was of indefinite age, perhaps in her seventies, thought Dorian Bayley. She hid her long, ruffled hair under a crumpled woollen cap, she was short and stocky, with a hollow, pale face. Her eyes were black as night and shone a strange vital light. She wore a mended but clean dress and wore homemade sandals on her feet.

'Please, Inspector Bayley, I've been waiting for you, come in, I've already put some water on the stove for tea,' she began with a kind smile and a calm voice.

'Has anyone announced my visit to you?'

Mrs Eleanor did not answer; she took two cups from a shelf, added some ground tea leaves and placed them on the table, together with a tray on which she served butter biscuits. When the teapot whistled, she grabbed it from the handle and filled the cups.

'I knew he'd visit me.'

'Then I guess you know why, too.'

'You are investigating the theft of an ancient manuscript and the subsequent disappearance of Inspector Nevil Morgan.'

'To which a murder has recently been added.'

'I heard,' the woman replied, whispering.

'Do you know Nevil Morgan?' the inspector asked after opening the notebook.

'I know many villagers; they come to me for advice or because they need comfort.'

'What kind of business do you profess?'

'You see, Inspector, not everyone understands that pain is part of life, that it must be accepted and overcome when it affects us. Many people are horrified by it and do everything they can to escape it, clinging to any handhold that can soothe or eliminate it. Those who come to me ask only this, and I try to make sure that they can process that pain and overcome it slowly.'

'Did Nevil Morgan ever ask you for help?'

'Inspector Morgan consults me on more complex cases when the laws of man alone prove insufficient.'

'Mrs Eleanor,' urged Dorian Bayley in a forceful tone, 'does the help you offer have anything to do with magic and foresight?'

The woman finished her tea by silently staring at the inspector. In her gaze, however, Dorian Bayley did not read a tone of challenge, but rather the need to understand.

'Let me make contact,' she replied, taking his right hand and resting it on hers with his palm facing upwards. 'You are a highly respected man; you have a fine intelligence that allows you to help so many people who have been wronged in life. By capturing the perpetrator of a crime you not only bring a criminal to justice but also ensure that the ethereal essence of the victim can find peace and leave the dimension in which he is imprisoned. Your acumen is profound, as is your ability. Yet your soul is wounded, a scar that you hide but always carry with you. And it is perhaps this secret that does not allow you to go beyond what you can perceive and to believe only in what is tangible and explainable by reason.'

A gust of wind slammed the door against the wall making a dull noise that made Bayley jump. The roar of thunder in the distance anticipated a blinding flash.

'Go now,' concluded Mrs Eleanor, leaving his hand and breaking contact, which had transmitted a strange warmth for the time it had been maintained.

'We haven't told each other everything yet,' he said before saying goodbye.

'Come back when you feel the need,' replied Mrs Eleanor while accompanying him on his way out.

The inspector waited until she had gone away; he took a few steps and stopped immediately after resuming the path. He opened his notebook and wrote:

Reticent in talking about Nevil Morgan / she professes to be a healer; charismatic, probably a charlatan / is she hiding something too?

***

A strong oblique wind forced him to shelter his face inside the lapel of his coat. He plunged his hands into his pockets and began to walk at a rapid pace. He had accumulated enough material to make the first deductions and decided to return to the police station rather than return to his quarters. In the evening, he would treat himself to a hot meal at the Count's inn. When he reached the edge of a small creek he stopped, as if stunned by whiplash. The wood seemed to come to life at that moment; its voice crept through the branches whistling and howling, while a thousand skeletal arms swayed threateningly suspended in the air. Dorian Bayley looked in every direction; he felt a clear presence nearby, as if someone were hiding in the trees and watching him in the shadows. For the first time since he was in *Greystone* he pulled out his revolver, ready to use it if that latent danger, which he perceived as a vague feeling of anxiety, had turned into something concrete.

'Someone has been following me ever since I left Mrs Eleanor's property,' he whispered to himself as he walked back. A thunder made him almost jump; a few seconds and a flash of lightning pierced the darkness, illuminating the silhouette of a being who was a few steps away from him. Dorian Bayley ordered him to stop, pointing his gun and extending his arm, ready to shoot. He approached the tree behind which he had seen him disappear. He seemed to him a tall, massive man, just as, from the assumptions made, he must have been Vernon Doyle's killer. The inspector's breathing became laboured; he moved with circumspection, taking care not to be taken by surprise. When he heard the roar of a new thunder, he prepared to leap to the other side of the trunk. He had calculated that less than five seconds elapsed between the noise and the next flash. When he counted three in his mind, he planted his left foot on the ground and leveraged himself to jump about two steps to the right. He grabbed the kick of the revolver with force, holding all the muscles of his arm taut. The light projected enough light to illuminate all around. Whoever was, had managed to escape, taking advantage of the darkness and the snowfall that had intensified to the point of making it difficult to see a few steps away. He managed to find his way back to the main path and, after about forty minutes, he came out of it near the wooden bridge. He stopped to catch his breath; he cleaned himself up from the snow and went without delay to the police station where, first, he lit the stove, prepared a hot tea and cut a cigar. Although nothing of interest had emerged from the conversation with Mrs Eleanor, the strange encounter in the woods convinced him that he was on the right track. He had confirmation that the murderer was still in *Greystone*.

***

'Men don't stop giving information until after they're buried. They speak as sick, drunk and even dead.'
This was often said by Roland Osborne, an old Scotland Yard instructor, who had contributed to Dorian Bayley's training in his early years. Never before have his aphorisms come so useful to rekindle the flame of an investigation that needed a shudder so as not to become discouraged under the ashes of mystery that surrounded *Greystone* and permeated the souls of its inhabitants. In fact, the most significant information he had in his hand had been the result of too many beers; for this reason, if he wanted to walk at least a small path that would lead him to the resolution of the case and return to his wife in London within two weeks, he felt he had to give credit to the words of George Davies. Then, if his nose had led him in the right direction, when the investigation was over he would personally thank "that damned Tom Porter" as the blacksmith had reproached, buying a supply of beer to take home.
'That clever man owes me at least five days' rest as soon as I get back to London,' he thought, referring to Paul Carter, as he walked back and forth in his office.
At that moment he heard a knock.
'Come on in, Jacob.'
The young officer came in with a scruffy look, as he had not announced himself verbally and did not understand how the inspector could see him.

'I have some information to give you, Inspector, but first there's Father Beathan who'd like to talk to you.'

'Let him in, then, when you see him leave, come back with Gordon.'

The priest entered with a copy of the Bible under his arm and a handkerchief in his hand, with which he had just dried his forehead. He was curious how he could sweat when the temperature outside was barely above zero.

'Good morning Inspector,' began with a worried tone of voice, 'I don't know if this is important information but this morning, entering the sacristy immediately after the service, I noticed that the second set of keys had disappeared. Therefore, I preferred to run to warn you immediately.'

'You did well, Father. Are you sure they were still in place last night, coming out of the church?'

The priest raised his eyes to the sky.

'I think so, but if I had to be sure, I don't know. It's not something I pay much attention to.'

Dorian Bayley got up to walk the priest to the door and, in a confidential tone, said to him:

'Father, I would ask you to keep your information to yourself and your eyes open.'

'You may rest assured, Inspector; I'll tell the deacon I took them home for safety. No one else may enter the sacristy without my permission.'

'Go back to your congregation and don't worry. As soon as I find out anything, I'll let you know.'

'Thank you, Inspector; if you like, I'll see you at mass on Sunday.' Father Beathan said goodbye, dabbing the sweat of his brow with a handkerchief.

Dorian Bayley left the door half open to avoid new knock-knock. That morning he hadn't woken up in a good mood; he still hadn't had time to devote himself to his ritual, and every little noise entered his head, amplifying itself as if it were the big bass drum.

Not even two minutes later Jacob Young peeked out again. His red hair, always perfectly arranged, was out of tune with the often confused way of presenting the facts and with a perennial and flashy sense of unease that the inspector found almost amusing.

The officer stopped in front of the desk, standing silently upright.

'I don't need to give you permission even to talk,' the inspector said.

Jacob Young implied a smile and handed him a report.

'I asked around and more than one person remembered seeing a stranger wandering around the village in the last few days. Everyone agrees with the physical appearance or, at least, the various descriptions seem to converge. He is a man with brown hair, in his fifties, not too tall, with a moustache and thick sideburns; he always wears elegant clothes, with a cape, top hat and walking stick. After the murder, he seems to have disappeared.'

'He may have left *Greystone*. Have you spoken to the station employees?'

'Gordon took care of that.'

'Anything else?'

'Little else,' he added, disappointed. He had come in convinced he had important information, but noted that the inspector's expression had not changed a bit.

'Now that I remember,' he read quickly in his notes, 'a farmer named Albert told me that he saw Adam Ford walking along a path through the woods, in the upper part of the village, just beyond the old wooden bridge.'

'And is that unusual?' asked Dorian Bayley as he alternated a sip of tea with a mouthful of cigar.

'I'd say yes,' Jacob replied, 'Albert had just left the pub, let's say he'd been kicked out by the owner; before going home he wanted to take a walk to sober up. As he walked past the church he read the time on the big clock; it was just after three o'clock. The time coincides, confirmed to me by the owner of the inn who, let's say, accompanied him to the door because he had to close it. The farmer kept walking until he crossed the wooden bridge, then he sat down to smoke and it was in those minutes that he saw Adam Ford. As far as I can tell, the cemetery caretaker was walking at a fast pace, he was wearing a hooded cape and it seemed to him that he was carrying something to his belt, even if he couldn't be more precise. All this happened the night between the 20th and 21st, the night Vernon Doyle was killed.'

'A careful observer,' exclaimed Dorian Bayley, who added immediately afterwards, 'even too much, since the scene took place in the middle of the night in a dimly lit area and has as its protagonist a witness who was standing by chance.'

'I'm just letting you know what I heard.'

'You're doing a great job; keep scouring the village. And, tell me, has Adam Ford ever had any trouble with the law?'

'I don't know; though he looks a bit gloomy, he's never committed any crime...'

Bayley stared at him with an inquisitive air.

'...as far as I know.' hurried to add the agent.

At that moment, Gordon Craig entered and took his place in front of the desk.

'What news do you bring me?' the inspector asked as he finished his tea.

'I went to the inn where Darrel Bennet stayed and asked to speak to the maid who was in charge of tidying his room. She remembered him well because he had left her a nice tip and so she described him to me in great detail. Afterwards I headed towards the train station and an attendant told me that he saw a distinguished man waiting for the train. I had him described to me and there's no doubt about it, it was Darrel Bennet.'

Bayley stared at him and, with a nod, invited him to move on.

'It was the late morning of last Tuesday, 21 October; from what he remembers, the man was dressed in a long dark coat of excellent workmanship. He took the twelve o'clock train from *Greystone* to *Little Castle*. The man seemed calm; he asked him how long the train would take, and then he got on it, at which point he never saw him again.'

Bayley thought that despite his young age and the fact that he had moved to *Greystone* with the intention of not putting too much effort into his work, Craig showed brilliance. He exposed what happened without having to read any notes, remembering everything by heart and, above all, he was witty in asking the station employee his impressions of Darrel Bennet.

'*Where is Little Castle?*'

'It's a small town 35 miles from here. It is connected to *Greystone* by a secondary railway line that opened last year. At the moment, two freight trains pass through it every day, carrying mainly grazing animals and building materials. Before they opened the new route, they had to take a carriage that took almost three hours to get there, but now it only takes a little more than one.

Dorian Bayley pulled his watch out of his pocket. It was 12:30.

'And you'll take the 4:00 p.m. today,' he announced without hesitation, 'you'll sleep there and as soon as you hear from him, I hope by tomorrow, you'll take the first train to *Greystone.*'

'Perfect Inspector.'

'As for you Jacob,' continued the inspector, staring the other officer in the eye, 'you should follow Adam Ford. Follow him all day today, never let him out of your sight and above all, don't get caught.'

'It will be a problem, Inspector. Everyone here at *Greystone* knows me.'

Dorian Bayley shook his head.

'Take off your uniform and put on your coat and hat. As long as there's light, you'll keep your distance. You'll be one man among many who walks the country on his day of rest. In the dark, it'll be easier.'

'Well, inspector.'

When the two officers left, Dorian Bayley sat back, undecided whether to study and reorder the clues collected or return to the crime scene to look for new elements.

'No crime can be solved by sitting down,' he thought, recalling another lecture by Roland Osborne.

He took another look at his watch, put on his coat and hat and headed for the door. Then he went back, opened the desk drawer, took the gun, put it in his pocket and went out.

***

Father Beathan never seemed to rest. When you met him, he was always busy taking care of some business. If he wasn't in church preparing for Sunday service or giving an audience to anyone in need, he would go around the village giving advice, helping a poor woman carry wood or playing with the children, running with them or hiding waiting to be found. If you wanted to talk to him, the only place not to look for him was his house, which he used only to sleep at night.

When he arrived near the library, Dorian Bayley saw him bent over in the small vegetable garden cleaning the snow from his plants, which were in danger of dying burnt by the ice.

'Inspector, what a pleasure,' he waved loudly with his usual benevolent smile.

The sleeves of the sweater were pulled up, while the pants were tied at the knees to protect them from the ground.

'Hello, Father. It's nice to meet you. I came to have a look in the library.'

'Give me a moment and I'll come to open it for you. You know, since Vernon left us, I can't keep the door open anymore.'

The inspector nodded to him and began searching the perimeter. He stopped to look at the remains of the stone walls that had once supported a paleo Christian temple. They seemed to be placed at random but, on careful analysis, it was clear that each of them tended to make a curve; the ancient temple seemed to have had a circular plan, while the small internal walls divided the space into small cells. Dorian Bayley ignored the function they might have had, although it was not difficult to imagine their votive use.

'This way, Inspector,' called the priest standing at the door.

Dorian Bayley approached and together they entered the library.

'Did you find out anything about the missing keys?' he asked as he widened the curtains to let the light in.

'Not at the moment, but we'll know something more precise soon.'

'I suppose you'd like to stay just to pursue your investigation. When you're done, I'll be at the church. I have some things to sort out for Sunday's service.'

'Thank you, Father, you are always precious to me.'

He accompanied the priest to the corridor leading to the sacristy, then closed the door behind him and observed the environment as if it were the first time.

'How did the killer get out if the doors were locked from the inside?' He wondered as he searched palm to palm the entire surface of the room. The L shape guaranteed several blind spots and a cunning killer would have an easy time assaulting an unsuspecting victim; moreover, the darkness of the night created the most formidable of hiding places. But the inspector's woodworm obsessively returned to the escape route used by the criminal. No windows showed signs of burglary, and there were no lofts to suggest an escape from the roof. As he felt the resistance of the large shelves containing the bookshelves, the most unlikely of ideas came to him, which he tried to erase from his mind for fear of turning the case into something grotesque. He began to touch the books at random, bending them at 45 degrees, as if looking for a hidden switch, pressing at the interstices that separated the shelves by a few inches. Even so, their weight would have made it impossible to hide a secret door. He repeated the operation until he came close to the end wall of the room, hidden by two large shelves, each taking up half the space, and ending almost merging with each other. The interior space was arranged as if a slightly smaller shelf were set into the larger one, and so on. On these too, the inspector tried every kind of pressure or movement to see if there could be a secret exit somewhere. The inspection, however, failed and Dorian Bayley blamed himself for only thinking he could listen to his imaginative side. When he turned to head for the sacristy, however, he heard something rubbing against the sole of a shoe. He knelt down and felt the floor with his fingers. In one very precise spot he found remains of the same soil discovered near the corpse, of a different consistency and colour from the one surrounding the church and the garden. The soil ended up just below the base of the shelf. Perhaps, Dorian Bayley thought, the murderer must have picked it up under the soles of his shoes somewhere else and, in the excitement of the murder, he must have lost it in two places: one where he had stopped waiting to reach the sacristy and the second in the spot near the crucifix where he had hidden himself to ambush him. He wiped his fingers and made his way to the sacristy. He called Father Beathan, then crossed the room and headed towards the altar. During the first inspection, he hadn't realized how beautiful the church was, adorned with Christian symbols and embellished with frescoes that covered the ceilings of the naves. Next to the large crucifix, moved to the right, a small altar collected the tabernacle that contained a gold chalice, an enamelled paten, the pyx also gold-plated and two small ampoules for wine. A little further back there was a pretty frame with shiny glass containing a hand-engraved symbol on a black background. Dorian Bayley took it to look at it better in the light.

'The Anglican rose,' began when Father Beathan suddenly appeared behind his back.

'Forgive me, Father, I shouldn't have touched,' the inspector apologized.

'On the contrary, I'm glad you take an interest in our congregation. The horror of what has happened must not undermine the beauty of the house of the Lord and, indeed, it must instil in us the courage necessary to search firmly for the truth and the word of God. What you hold in your hand is an ancient symbol of communion, as well as being the coat of arms on which all the Anglican churches can be recognized. 'Look in the centre,' he said, pointing to an inscription that made a full circle around a white circle in the centre of the blue rose, 'is an inscription in Latin and means *The truth will set you free*, John 18:12-20. These are words spoken by our Lord Jesus when He came to Jerusalem. And I know that, in his heart, you too are seeking the truth.'

'I wish I had your ardour, Father, to believe in something beyond that, but right now, the only truth I'm looking for is the perpetrator of a murder.'

'God's love comes in different forms; God loves you like all his children. But I don't want to keep you any longer. I know you have a lot of work to do.'

'I'll come back and warn you when I've discovered something. Now excuse me,' said Dorian Bayley.

As he left the church, he was accompanied by the feeling that something was eluding him even though he had it under his nose, the same strange feeling that had struck him during the inspection in Nevil Morgan's house.

25 October 1884 – Saturday

Gordon Craig had never visited *Little Castle*, although the village was only a few miles from where he served. He imagined it not very different from *Greystone*, a village surrounded by woods and hills with a square in the centre, a church, small shops and a few pubs to console himself from the daily grind. As soon as he set foot at his destination, he thought he hadn't made much of a mistake but, after an hour, he already felt he was living in a completely different atmosphere; poorer, more sober and simpler. The streets, even the central ones, were poorly lit and the people who still crowded the streets at 6 p.m. were wearing worn out clothes and roughly stitched shoes. The sturdy two-storey houses were built of stone, with two windows per floor and sloping roofs. The snow that had fallen in the previous days persisted piled up on the sides of the cobblestone paved alleys; in some places it had not been carefully shovelled and, turning to ice, had made the ground slippery. What was not missing was the wood: there was no garden or yard that did not contain large piles, the same ones that were well tidy outside the doors. The chimneys smoked without interruption, spreading a strong smell of burnt wood through the air, much more intense than what you could breathe in *Greystone*. *Little Castle* was famous for being above all an intensive coal mining area.

If his goal was to return the next day, there was no time to lose; he had to immediately set out in search of Darrel Bennet, challenging the pitfalls of cold and slippery roads. From a station attendant he had managed to get information about the places in the village that would be useful to him: the pubs and the church, classic meeting places, the market, which was only held on Sunday mornings, the police headquarters and, not to mention the inns that housed strangers. Here, too, there were only two and they bore the names of the species most present in the area: *The Pine* and *The Oak*. They were a short distance from each other; the first was in the centre of Tree Pine Square, while the second overlooked a street connected to it which, ironically, bore the name of Killing Street.

If the residents of *Greystone* were little used to seeing strangers pass through the streets of the village, thought Gordon Craig, the residents of *Little Castle* should have been even more intrigued to see a new face; however, it seemed that his presence went unnoticed. He noticed, indeed, that some of the elders hinted a greeting with their heads as if they were expecting his visit. So as not to look like an officer on duty, Craig had also given up his official uniform to wear a heavy wool cape, thick dark green trousers, and a pair of leather ankle boots. He soon arrived in Pine Tree square and entered the first inn, where a maid with a kind smile and a good-looking face greeted him. As he was about to ask the names of the guests who were staying there he was distracted by a frenzied rumour coming from one of the alleys that branched off the square towards the northern part of the village; he apologized to the maid and, intrigued, went to check what was happening. He stopped in front of an entrance illuminated by two oil lamps; he entered and found himself inside what at first glance looked like a small shop. Positioned in a row of four, divided by a corridor that opened in the middle, there were twenty red velvet chairs, insufficient to hold everyone present; some men had had to be content to stand on either side of the room. When stepped into the room, a strong smell of cigar attacked Gordon Craig's nostrils. He found a space, standing next to a short, thin but well-dressed man, intent on being inconspicuous. The bystanders, all men of various ages dressed in elegant, controlled posture, spoke to each other and exchanged opinions. At the end of the room, on a long table placed sideways, were placed ancient objects of various kinds, all classified with a label showing the period, the name and the basic value: work tools, clothes, parts of furniture, paintings, jewellery and much more. Craig realized he was in the middle of an auction and discreetly observed those present to see if anyone matched Darrel Bennet's description. From a booth at the back, without any announcement, came out the auctioneer, a man dressed in black with a short tie and a moustache upwards, holding a cigar case that Craig thought might be gold-plated.

'We welcome the young gentleman at the end of the hall,' he announced in a ceremonial tone, pointing to Gordon Craig, as everyone present turned to observe him.

'Damn,' he thought irritated, 'it doesn't seem the best way to go unnoticed.'

The agent gathered all the nonchalance he had already shown in the past to get out of uncomfortable situations like that. He took a half step forward and took a bow.

'Good evening, everybody,' he said with a big smile, 'I'm ready to give battle.'

Among those present, composed giggles were raised, and the auctioneer started the new auction.

No one seemed interested in the proposed object. The next item, a Florentine teapot in fine porcelain of the seventeenth century, was instead sold after just three raises at a price slightly higher than the basic price. It soon moved on to what must have been one of the highlights of the evening, which proved to attract the attention of bystanders. It was a 16th century painting from Serbia, depicting a zoomorphic demon, painted half man and half goat, who held a woman prisoner, while all around the trees came to life and stretched their branches threateningly towards the two protagonists, almost undecided whether to stand in defence of the woman or submit to the will of the demon. Craig was not a connoisseur of art, but he felt a strong emotional charge generated by the painting, as if it were able to convey gloomy emotions.

An animated auction began and, among the most active bidders, Gordon Craig recognized the man he was looking for. He was sitting in the second row in a perfectly cut dark suit. He was holding his stick in the armrest of his chair and a dull pipe in his hand. He seemed at ease and knew how to enter his offers discreetly but with refined skill, often a moment before he seemed to want to give up.

'He's trying to discourage other buyers,' he thought admired.

After about the raises he managed to win the painting for the incredible sum, so the agent valued it at £110. Those present gave a thunderous applause and the man stood up, showing two large moustaches and important long sideburns, making a warm bow of thanks. Walking with his stick, he walked up to the auctioneer and signed a big tome on the desk. At that moment Craig had no more doubts: it was Darrel Bennet. The young agent had a gasp when he realized that the suspect had held the pen in his left hand.

After signing, Bennet was seated in the back to complete the sale and purchase transactions. When he returned to the room he walked towards the coat rack, resting on the wall opposite the one where Craig was staying, put on his coat and top hat and left the room.

'Is he trying to escape?' Craig asked himself, fearing he'd be discovered when the auctioneer pointed at him loudly.

Without a second's thought, he jumped out of the room. The clean air awakened him but the cold became even more pungent, forcing him to lift his lapel and put on gloves. Darrel Bennet walked quickly to the main square, where the inn was located. Gordon Craig thought to chase him and grab him in the street, but then chose to follow him without being seen. At that moment, Tree Pine Square was desolate. It was dinnertime and people were huddled in their homes; the smell of burning wood coming out of the chimneys had mixed with the smell of roasted food.

In an attempt not to take too much distance from Bennet, he accelerated his pace but put his foul foot on a slab of ice and fell to the ground ruinously. Bennet heard the noise, turned around and realized he was being followed. He fled down a lane that branched off to the south from the square. Cursing the ice that had betrayed him, the young officer got up and, despite a sore arm, chased him with all his breath. He saw him enter the inn called *The Oak;* within a short while he found himself inside too. He was caught talking to the innkeeper who was sitting behind a wooden desk, with a rather compromised appearance, in the small hall from which the steps leading to the upstairs rooms went up.

'You stop, don't move,' he told him with a broken breath.

'Who are you?' the owner of the inn intervened.

Craig took a breath and took his badge out of his pocket.

'Officer Gordon Craig,' he said, spelling out the words, 'the gentleman here is in custody and is now coming with me.'

The innkeeper instantly abandoned the tone of challenge.
'At your command,' he whispered in a quiet tone.
'You may also remove the sign *rooms sold out,* the gentleman will sleep at the local police station and come to *Greystone* with me tomorrow.'
'But the gentleman is not my guest,' replied the innkeeper with an air of perplexity.
Darrel Bennet seemed incapable of uttering a word. He was amazed, as if a bucket of cold water had rained down on him.
'Follow me,' Craig told him, 'you owe us quite a bit of explanation.'
When they left Killing Street to cross the square again it was just after eight o'clock at night.

26 October 1884 – Sunday

The train to *Greystone* had left on time at 10 a.m. and by 11.20 a.m. it had reached its destination quay, where merchants and farm workers were already busy loading food, animal feed, milk supplies and even two cows to be transported to *Little Castle* at noon.
Darrel Bennet had not spent a quiet night, although he had preferred not to show it during the trip; he had kept a calm and demeanour that did not befit a man in custody. He had tried to ask Gordon Craig for more information about the accusations made against him, even though he knew in his heart what they would challenge him. The officer, however, said nothing; he had been instructed to take the suspect to Inspector Dorian Bayley and not to carry out a preliminary interrogation, let alone provide information that would help Bennet prepare a line of defence. He had chosen not to handcuff him, believing it unlikely that the man would prevail in an escape attempt or hand-to-hand combat.
As they walked along the dock, Craig caught a glimpse of George Davies; the blacksmith was negotiating with an acquaintance about the method and price of selling some of the handles, which were most likely on their way to *Little Castle*. The officer knew that he had been the first to report to the inspector that he had seen Darrel Bennet wandering around the village near the church, and he found it amusing to see how the coincidences seemed to play dice with people's fate.
When they arrived at the office they found the thoughtful inspector holding a telegraphed sheet of paper in his hand.

It was information about Darrel Bennet that Scotland Yard had recently sent over. With the paper in his hand he waved the two of them in and closed the door behind them.

'Thanks, Gordon, great job,' he said to his agent as he invited him to sit at the side of the desk.

'Mr Bennet, I am Inspector Dorian Bayley of Scotland Yard and I must ask you a few questions and ask you to answer them truthfully if you do not wish to aggravate your position.'

'That's why I'm here,' replied Bennet, removing the cylinder and carefully placing it on a coat rack, where the stick also ended up hanging. He seemed impassive and controlled every gesture very carefully. When he placed the chair, he took care not to drag it, but lifted it just off the floor, making it stick to the floor without causing the slightest noise. He unbuttoned his coat and watched his shirt, disappointed that it was not flawless; the night before, while Craig was waiting for him to take him to the police station, he had failed to check again that everything was in order.

'Your name is Darrel Bennet, you are 52 years old and from Manchester. You are a wealthy man and an art lover but, at the same time, works for Sir Donald Acton, also a famous collector but with financial means and political support far superior to yours. There are no serious offences against you but, about three years ago, you were accused of bribing an auctioneer for an antique.'

Dorian Bayley had decided to get right to the point and tackle the issues by getting to the heart of the matter without going around it.

'It was a Breton shield dating back to the seventh century,' Bennet replied quietly, 'and I am pleased to tell you that I was fully acquitted of that shameful accusation.

I have also made the exhibit available to several museums who have requested it free of charge.'

'We also know this,' hurried to add the inspector who did not stop staring the suspect in the eye, 'and we also know that Sir Acton, in addition to a deep passion for antiques, is fascinated by esotericism and uses you as an intermediary to find books and objects that are thought to have magical power; just like the manuscript that disappeared from Adam Ford's house, stolen the same day of your arrival in *Greystone*. What can you tell me about that?'

Under Darrell Bennet's big moustache, an annoyed smile grew.

'I'm a gentleman, and if you've taken information about me anyone could have confirmed it. Could a man in my position ever break into someone else's house? I'm sorry, Inspector, but the thought of it offends me.'

Dorian Bayley was on the line between irritation and surprise. The suspect was certainly not familiar with police interrogations and the night before was forced, for the first time in his life, to spend the night locked in a cell. He had been coercively picked up and taken to *Greystone* and now he was the object of insinuations difficult for a member of his social class to tolerate. However, he didn't break down at all and his only concern seemed to be the pleats on his shirt.

'No, in fact, I find that hard to believe, but I didn't say that...' confirmed the inspector ready to launch another round, 'you may have commissioned someone local and, if so, your old corruption charge might whisper something in my ear...'

The collector was ready to reply but Dorian Bayley anticipated him.

'We know you were acquitted, you already told me. But do you know how many wrongful acquittals I've seen over the years?'

'I must deduce, Inspector, that you did not trouble me from my engagements at *Little Castle* to ask me any questions, but to offend me; know that I find these allegations most repugnant.'

Once again, the tone of voice did not show the slightest hint of anger.

'Don't be sorry,' the inspector urged him in a good-natured manner, 'I'm only carrying out an investigation and it mortifies me to know that my deductions offend you. However, and I tell you this in all sincerity, Mr Bennet, experience suggests to me that this whole story is dragging on a trail of mystery from which it is hard to believe that you are completely unconnected.'

Without further ado, the inspector turned to Gordon Craig to ask him how he'd managed to track down the suspect in *Little Castle*. The officer spoke with the usual clarity, once again without the need to consult notes, while Dorian Bayley wrote it all down in his notebook shaking his head from time to time, more emphatically when the officer recounted that Darrel Bennet, at the sight of him, had fled in a hurry.

For the first time the art dealer's face appeared tense.

'You see, sir,' the inspector took up the same tone with which a patient teacher teaches life to his apprentice, 'who flees always has something to hide. And what did you have to hide?'

'The explanation is very simple: I was afraid.'

'Afraid of what?'

'I travel the United Kingdom to deal with the purchase and sale of rare, often very expensive pieces, and I always carry a large sum of money with me. Imagine, Inspector, the reaction I had when I realised I was being followed in the evening by a stranger after an auction in which I had bought a painting worth more than most people can earn by working all their lives.'

'And tell me, Mr Bennet,' urged the inspector who wanted to play like a cat with a mouse, 'why did you not go to the inn where you were staying, but to another?'

'Actually I was on my way to that very inn, because in the village it's the only place where you can telegraph a message, even if for a large payment. I had to warn Sir Acton that I had won the painting; he had been after it for years and would pay anything to see it in his collection.'

Darrel Bennet seemed to have an answer to every objection, but Dorian Bayley had hidden two tricks up his sleeve and decided it was time to throw them on the table.

'And I suppose it is also a coincidence that you left *Greystone* on the morning of 21 October, a few hours after the murder of the Church librarian,' he exclaimed with a veil of sarcasm.

'I had arranged appointments at *Little Castle*, where an antiques week was planned, with specially organised auctions and fairs. I had certain information that, among goods of dubious taste, I would find some extremely interesting pieces. There was also a rumour that *The Lady with the Demon* would be auctioned off these very days. I was not fleeing and had nothing to do with the murder, which I learned the next day by talking to the innkeeper at breakfast.'

Dorian Bayley noted down the statements, then resumed.

'So, I guess it's normal to book a room until 26 October paying the full amount and leave on the 21st without notifying the owner.'

Bennet slipped two fingers on his big moustache.

'Inspector, if you hadn't forcibly anticipated my return, I would have returned to *Greystone* tomorrow and then left on the 26th for Manchester. That's why I left the room booked. As for the paid and unused days, my employer does not care about such matters, which are trifling in relation to the main purpose of my travels. His financial resources are enormous and he often acts in a way that makes him seem careless, but it is only a matter of opportunism.'

'And what did you come to *Greystone* for? I am not aware that there should be any auctions,' the inspector resumed, beginning to hammer more decisively. 'I tell you with the utmost sincerity, Mr Bennet, we suspect that only one object might be of interest to you: the manuscript stolen from Adam Ford. Because, contrary to popular belief, I remain convinced that it is of immense value.'

'It is true, Inspector, there are no auctions or antiques events in *Greystone,* but Sir Acton is a well-known fan of esotericism, as you have just confirmed. Around this village there are rumours of strange phenomena, not always identified, which occur with a certain frequency. We are talking about apparitions, séances, evocations of dead souls. I had come to check how real it was, being *Greystone,* moreover, an almost obligatory passage to reach *Little Castle*.'

'And what would you find out about these phenomena?'

'It's hard to see straight, but it seems people are scared and prefer not to say much. There are legends and superstitions that can be the object of study for enthusiasts, but a few days are not enough to interpret their dynamics and deepen their contents. Maybe one day I'll come back to study this aspect better. The fact is that the main objective of this trip was the purchase of the painting in *Little Castle*.'

'Mr. Bennet,' resumed Dorian Bayley in a strong tone, 'you were seen walking near the church the day before Vernon Doyle was murdered. Apart from all your lucubration about art and esotericism, can you imagine how delicate your position is, or do you still want us to believe you can sleep soundly?'

'What can I tell you, Inspector. Where does an art lover go when he goes to a country he's never seen before?'

Bayley didn't move a muscle and kept staring him right in the eye, so Bennet continued.

'The church is always a place of deep artistic interest. St. Patrick's is no less and the inhabitants of this village should be proud to host a masterpiece of historical and architectural importance like this one.'

The inspector finished noting the answers, then got up and went to the window, staring into the distance at the high hills, where huge piles of black clouds were gathering.

'A storm is about to hit the town,' thought Dorian Bayley with a clear metaphorical reference.

Soon the facts would prove him right.

'If you have no further questions, Inspector, I'd like to go and rest.'

'Craig, escort the gentleman to the basement; he will stay here under visual surveillance.' ordered Dorian Bayley facing the officer, who had followed the interrogation very closely.

'Mr Bennet,' he said, finally turning his back on the collector on his way to the door, 'you will not leave *Greystone* until further notice.'

The inspector came out slamming the door behind him, deliberately giving the impression of being angry. As soon as he came out, he opened his notebook again and wrote a footnote at the bottom of the notes:

– He's lying about why he really came to *Greystone* –

***

Towards evening, sneezes were heard coming from the corridor. Dorian Bayley peeked through the door left half closed and saw Jacob Young trembling in front of the burning stove as he tried to warm himself by rubbing his hands and breathing vehemently on it. He was wearing his service uniform but had a huge wool scarf around his neck. The inspector prepared a cup of tea and pour boiling water, leaving it steaming on the desk.

'Is this stove working?' he asked the young officer, pointing to the one in his office.

As he sat in the chair in front of the desk he nodded yes with his head; he held the cup tightly in his hands, and began to sip tea, trying to warm his hands and stomach.

'I guess it was a long stakeout,' began Dorian Bayley as he took two logs of wood from the pile and put them in the stove.

Before starting to speak, Jacob sipped the tea again, eventually emitting a sigh of satisfaction. He thanked the inspector and took the inseparable notebook from his pocket.

'I followed your instructions to the letter, Inspector. I left home around 4p.m. yesterday afternoon and headed for the Golden pub, where I drank a beer and exchanged a few chats with the waiter at the counter. I gave the impression I was there to enjoy the day off. I had a look around but I didn't notice anything relevant. By then the place was almost deserted. After about an hour or so I went out and started walking around the village; there were few people around, it was very cold and the sun was almost setting. I headed for the cemetery and, with the excuse of visiting an uncle who is buried there, I exchanged a joke with Adam. He seemed calm and not at all surprised to see me. He was busy with his work, so I greeted and pretended to leave, while I lurked along a side path from where I could keep an eye on the entrance without being seen. The suspect stayed in his place until 6:30p.m., when he closed the cemetery gate and headed home. I followed him from afar and stopped to spy on him from the back windows of the house. After dinner, his wife and son went upstairs while he sat in the living room and had a drink. He checked his watch several times and the more time went by, the more nervous he got. At a certain moment he started looking for something, I don't know what, but I saw that he was opening drawers and shop windows moving objects and various trinkets. And then he went upstairs and turned off the lights.'

'What time could it be?'

'I was watching the clock; it was just after ten. I confide to you, Inspector, that the cold had become very stinging, and I began to tremble like a leaf even though I was wearing my heaviest coat, woollen hat, and gloves on my hands. You had told me to follow his movements until evening, and I was almost about to leave, for I was sure he had gone to bed, or else the light came on again in the drawing room before midnight; it was Adam. I could tell by the way he was dressed that he was getting ready to go out. He took a belt with what I think was his hunting knife from a padlocked wardrobe. Adam has never made a mystery of being a hunting enthusiast and, whenever he has the chance, he gets lost in the woods in search of some prey to take home. Of course, I was surprised that he wanted to go out at that time of night and in wolf weather like that. So I continued the stakeout.'

'What time did he leave?'

'After about 20 minutes. It was like he was waiting for a specific time to do it, like he had an appointment.'

'And did your feelings turn out to be correct?'

Jacob felt proud to have captured the attention of his superior. The heat that was starting to come out of the stove made the environment pleasant.

'Yes, Inspector. Adam went out guarded and headed along the path that leads into the woods behind the cemetery. He passed a small road that leads to St Patrick's Square, the brook at a little-known spot where there are the old ruins of a bridge dating back to Roman times and came out of the woods near a mule track halfway between the church and Judge Owen's villa.'

'That's interesting. Was someone waiting for him?'

'This is where the weirdness begins, Inspector. Adam Ford approached the library and waited for someone who showed up shortly afterwards. But it was not one person, but two: Mayor Montgomery Chapman and Judge Frank Owen.'

'Are you sure?' Dorian Bayley asked in amazement.

'Absolutely, it was them,' replied the officer confidently.

A long silence followed the enunciation of the two names. To connect three men who apparently had no connection between them and, moreover, to do so late at night near the place where a crime had taken place, seemed to the inspector an extremely important issue to be included in the investigation. He did not want to draw hasty conclusions, but the case was taking an unexpected turn.

'Keep going,' he simply said.

'They spoke a few minutes in a low voice; I was too far away, and could not hear anything they said to each other; but they seemed to be exchanging instructions for action. It was above all Judge Owen who was giving directions by flailing and pointing as if they had a mental map to follow. Afterwards they lifted the hoods of the capes that all three of them were wearing and headed for the library door, which they opened with a key.'

'That's where Father Beathan's stolen keys went,' Bayley thought puzzled.

'I had hidden behind a tree a few meters away but the curtains were all drawn and, from that moment, I could only see shadows. They had lit candles and walked around the room for a long time. The way they were moving, I could swear they were looking for something.'

'And you think they found it?'

'Unfortunately, I haven't been able to understand much. One of the three of them lay down on the ground, I didn't see him for a while, then got up and shortly afterwards headed for the exit locking the door. While they were inside, I heard noises as if they were moving the desks and chairs, nothing else.'

'I wonder what they were looking for,' thought Dorian Bayley aloud, 'yet both Gordon and I searched the library inch by inch and I'm sure we missed nothing; but something must have been there if three men in the middle of the night risked that way to retrieve it.'

'I know Adam, Inspector, and I can assure you he's an honest man. As for the judge and the mayor, could they possibly be guilty of such a vicious crime? And if so, what is the point?'

'That's what we have to find out. You've been very precious Jacob; now go home, take a hot bath and rest. I'm going back to the inn, I still have work to do. I'll see you in the morning.'

'I'll be in and out,' smiled the officer, 'I'm on call tonight.'

'When this whole thing is over, you and Gordon have earned yourselves a rewarding vacation. By the way, do you know when Agent Lambert will be back?'

'He telegraphed just today; the doctors gave his mother a few days to live and he is the only son. But if you want I can write to him and call him back on duty.'

'No need; send him a telegram tomorrow and write to him that he can consider himself on leave for as long as he needs. You'll see that we'll manage all the same. Good night, Jacob.'

'Good night, Inspector.'

***

Late in the afternoon, coming out of the police station, Dorian Bayley noticed that he had been worn out from the long day. He also noticed that Agent Young's eyelids tended to droop and soon his eyes would close into a long, improvised sleep on the desk in the hallway. He was aware that he had put too much pressure on guys who were accustomed to resolving simple farmers' quarrels or stopping a few brawls outside the pubs, but the seriousness of the situation required a decisive and, above all, swift response. In London he could have counted on the support of at least twenty selected agents, while in *Greystone* much of the work had to be handled alone. He feared that the trail would start to go cold very soon.

He took the path to Main Street at a great pace. The main street was deserted and only from the inn you could hear isolated screams and a few songs crippled by alcohol. He looked up to the sky; he was pervaded by a feeling of strangeness never felt before. The clouds had thinned and the faint reflection of the stars filtered through like votive candles announcing the return of the dead in the night of Samhain. A faint reddish glow thickened almost invisibly on the horizon which, flashes in the distance, invigorated for a few moments. The air was full of mystery. Even the muffled sound of footsteps in the fresh snow created an imperceptible vibrating echo. It was not difficult for him to understand how such atmospheres could influence the minds of simple people, how it was almost logical to accept the existence of a supernatural dimension capable of explaining how the world works, rather than getting rid of what he thought to be simple suggestion and embrace a scientific vision of life. Dorian Bayley knew that superstition owed its radicalism to the sense of ancestral fear it was able to unleash. He understood how simple it was to introduce this feeling into the helpless minds of those who had to struggle every day to survive, fuelling fear with the anger and frustration of feeling inadequate and victims of an unjust and classist society. *Greystone* presented itself as a healthy and prosperous community. There was a school and the level of literacy was higher than the average in the rest of Great Britain. The role of the church also seemed instrumental in educating citizens and making them immune to mystical beliefs. Father Beathan was a rather progressive priest; he listened humbly to the problems of the faithful and preferred to give advice and practical help rather than use psychological advantage based on fear of divine punishment or horrific visions after death. But similar to a centuries-old oak tree with long branched roots in fertile soil, there was a hidden germ that permeated the air with a vague irrational essence, like a slow-absorption poison that descended from above causing the effect of an invisible and odourless hood that held the entire village captive. He felt its presence himself, small painless shocks that touched the sensitive nerves of his body. Vernon Doyle had been murdered by someone who had to have a precise motive, a murder based on the most classic of criminal schemes. Once the killer was discovered the case would be dismissed as one of many and he would return to London to resume his life. Every veil of superstition would melt like wax under the flame of truth, the only one Dorian Bayley knew, which burned fuelled by science and positivist thought.

When in the distance he heard noises disappearing from the pub, he had arrived near Kings Road; the lights of the houses overlooking the street were off and only in the distance you could see a small lamp that illuminated the sign of the inn where he was staying. The other two single streetlamps were drowsy at the entrance to the road. In the middle of the street he stopped as if he had a premonition. The silence was almost absolute and the darkness threatened every hidden corner. Dorian Bayley took his hands off the coat and slid them slowly along the buttons, ready to open it and pull out the revolver at the slightest suspicious movement. The moon was strewn with a veil of high, thin clouds and cast a faint ashy light. He resumed walking with circumspection, with cadenced steps, looking for the weak sources of light that appeared at random along the road. He heard a light rustling coming from behind a hedge; he pulled out the revolver and approached it pointing in that direction. Someone was hiding and about to jump out. Though with difficulty, he noticed that there were no tracks of any kind on the side of the road, so whoever it was must have come from the woods. Could it have been the killer who was wandering around the area waiting to find an opportunity to escape? Or was he continuing to hide nearby to complete the mission, as Dr Burlow theorized?

When he was a few steps away from the hedge, the rustle turned into a louder noise. With the palm of his left hand he shook the hand holding the revolver. He was undecided whether to fire a warning shot or move to surprise him from the side. On the horizon, a flash of bright red lit up the farthest part of the sky, which seemed to surround the high black hills surrounding the village in the south. A sudden leap, followed by a high-pitched hiss, almost made the inspector lose his balance, who managed to keep his nerves and his gun firmly in his hands. A moment before firing, he noticed a feline running away and disappearing into a side garden, jumping over a low fence. Dorian Bayley was unable to release the adrenaline that suddenly felt the footsteps behind him. He turned around, reached out his arm, but a well-aimed shot from someone hiding in the night blew his revolver out of his hand, which slipped and got lost in the hedges. In front of him he saw a man with a long black cloak and a raised hood covering his face. Vigorous arms held a loaded stick to strike again with the utmost ferocity. Unable to retrieve the weapon, he took up a defensive position and waited for the first move, which was not long in coming. With a rapid movement he managed to move to the right, avoiding that the weapon hit him on the head, but the snow and the icy road did not allow him to dodge the shot completely. The stick hit him hard on the shoulder, causing him to collapse to the ground. His enemy's behaviour was impetuous but poorly calculated. He had planned to catch him unawares and run away after a few seconds but, having failed the plan, he panicked, relying on improvisation and acting clumsily. Given his youthful boxing record, if he confronted him with his bare hands, Dorian Bayley thought, he might prevail. Without hesitation, he rolled to the left with the healthy shoulder. His analysis proved accurate. A deaf noise made him realize that the attacker had struck almost blindly, plunging the stick into the thick layer of snow. The inspector took advantage of this to make the reverse move; he endured the excruciating pain in his left shoulder and managed to grasp the blunt object, which was crushed under his belly after the enemy was forced to let go. He tried to get up with his right hand as he tried to grab the stick with the other hand, but the frozen ground made him slip on his knees and in turn made him lose his grip on the weapon; it was at that moment that he felt a sharp pain at the base of his skull. It was like sinking into a place without light. He remained in a suspended state where he felt his body float without any more weight, carried by a placid current that he felt flowing beneath him. He stopped thinking and allowed those enveloping sensations to infuse him with primordial energies whose origins were lost in the infinite flow of time.

When he opened his eyes, it took him a few seconds to focus on his surroundings and realize that he was lying on his bed; sitting next to them, he recognized the faces of Jacob and Gordon. He tried to stand up but a dizziness forced him to rest his head on the pillow.

'What happened?' he asked in a hoarse voice as he touched a tight bandage around his head.

Jacob stood up and approached the bed with his helmet in his hand.

'A waiter from the inn ran to the police station and told me that he had first heard noises and, immediately afterwards, helped a wounded man lying on the floor. When he realized it was you, together the owner took you to your room and called the doctor, who dressed your head.'

'How long has it been?'

'About two hours since they found you.'

Dorian Bayley's facial expression contorted in a grimace of pain. He felt like a vise was gripping his skullcap and his left shoulder was all sore.

'I only remember being attacked,' he began looking at the ceiling and swallowing with difficulty, 'I tried to defend myself but the assailant was faster and managed to hit me with something heavy. At that point he must have escaped, perhaps because he noticed the waiter who had come out of the inn called by the noises. His prompt intervention saved my life.'

Dorian Bayley half-closed his eyes trying to collect the memories that, in the meantime, resurfaced.

'Did you happen to find a stick?'

'Yes, it was under you. Whoever attacked you didn't have time to recover it.'

'And this reveals an important detail,' replied the inspector, as if he were just thinking out loud.

'If he preferred to flee rather than retrieve the stick, it is because he was afraid of being recognized; it is likely, therefore, that it is a local person,' continued Gordon Craig, demonstrating an uncommon wit.

Dorian Bayley nodded.

'But are we sure the man who tried to kill you is the same man who murdered Vernon Doyle?' Jacob Young asked.

'It is what we need to find out,' replied the inspector, 'but it is now established that more people, perhaps accomplices among them, are involved in this matter. Jacob, tomorrow I want to know if there is anyone in the village who is an expert in the antiquities trade. Now go and get some rest; I'll see you tomorrow evening at the police station to take stock of the situation.'

'It will be done,' assured Jacob while wearing his service helmet.

When the two officers left the room, Dorian Bayley got up, put water on the fire, made a cup of tea and started cutting a cigar. It was not the time to sleep; what he had to do was collect all the accumulated material and try to make sense of it.

27 October 1884 – Monday

'We are working on three fronts,' began Dorian Bayley, 'the first concerns the theft of the book in Adam Ford's house, the second the disappearance of Inspector Nevil Morgan and, finally, there is the murder of Vernon Doyle. It is now established that the three events are linked, although we still can't get to the bottom of it. That is why I have summoned you at this hour; darkness and silence are a factory of ideas.'
Agent Craig and Agent Young had been summoned to Dorian Bayley's office at 10:00 p.m. The initiative had been taken by the inspector, who wanted to put together the main clues gathered and start formulating more structured hypotheses about what happened at *Greystone*. The assault had tested him even though he hadn't suffered a fracture and his head was still sore; the urgency to solve the case, however, prevented him from wasting even a minute.
The day had gone by without too many jolts, with the inspector still recovering from the severe contusion that had knocked him out the night before.
Jacob Young had managed to get a message to a *Little Castle* art expert named Edmund Vinson, asking him to make an appointment for the next morning. The reply was not long in coming and a return telegram containing the address and time of the meeting was delivered to the agent within two hours, signed by Professor Vinson's secretary.
In regard to the state of the investigation, if on the one hand they had already identified two suspects on whom

there were rather serious clues, on the other hand there was nothing to link all the episodes that happened to one or more protagonists. A reasoned reading of the collected clues led to a series of questions that had not yet been answered. If Darrel Bennet was the murderer, who had attacked him near the inn, considering that he was in custody at the time? Could he have been an accomplice? And if so, what was his identity? If the perpetrator of the murder was Adam Ford instead, why did he risk being discovered in the middle of the night in the library with the likes of Judge Owen and Mayor Chapman?

'Before I even take stock of the situation, however,' continued Dorian Bayley after a long cigar pull, 'I must thank you very much for your dedication and commitment to this investigation. I don't suppose you're used to so much overtime around here, especially now that there are only two of you. But if there is one thing I am certain of in this country, where everything seems so cryptic and mysterious, it is that I can trust you.'

Jacob Young couldn't stand it any longer and rocked with his torso like a child about to put a chocolate cake in his mouth. The inspector, on the other hand, was a fine connoisseur of the human psyche before he was an irreducible bloodhound, which had earned him the esteem of the London police force, which rightly considered him one of its best detectives. He had learned how important it was to motivate his staff, the more complex the case appeared to be and he was able to skilfully modulate the level of tension to which they were subjected, alternating moments of frenetic commitment with others where one could indulge in a joke or a sip of tea.

Despite the cold that fogged up the window panes, the temperature inside the office was pleasant. Dorian Bayley had kept the stove alive all evening and the dry air was a blessing compared to the damp cold outside.

'Perhaps we're not dealing enough with the disappearance of Inspector Nevil Morgan,' Gordon Craig dared.

'So it seems,' replied Dorian Bayley, 'but, unless improbably lucky, I'm afraid that in order to put together the pieces of this puzzle we have to go back to the causes that determined this situation; personally I believe that the disappearance of Nevil Morgan is only a consequence.'

'Do you think he was murdered, Inspector?'

'Unfortunately, I think it's likely and, besides, the alternative would only be slightly better.'

'Meaning?' Craig asked.

'Which means he was involved in the disappearance of the book and the murder of Vernon Doyle, so let's put it this way: his death would prove his innocence, while any other case would greatly exacerbate his position.'

He was ready to accept the protests of the two officers who, instead, said nothing.

'These are the facts,' he continued by opening the notebook he had deposited on his desk.

'It all begins Monday, 13 October: Adam Ford, the cemetery caretaker, reports a book stolen from his home. It is an esoteric manuscript that seems to have little economic value. The case is being handled by Nevil Morgan himself, involving the entire police station as if it were a matter of the utmost importance.'

'That's right,' Jacob Young agreed.

'However, after five days, i.e. Saturday, 18 October, Nevil Morgan himself disappears into thin air. The last to see him, just the morning of the 18th, is Judge Frank Owen, his friend. When I questioned him, he couldn't tell me anything that would help me, like nobody else in the whole country.'

The two officers nodded.

'And here's the first oddity: Judge Owen is hiding something. He says he had no idea where Nevil Morgan was going the day he lost track of him, but maid Margaret confided in me that she was sure the inspector wasn't on his way to the police station, but was about to do some reconnaissance. An inspection which, in all probability, cost him dearly.'

Dorian Bayley got up from his desk feeling very dizzy but, ignoring the rules of the good detective, he pulled out of a locker door three small glasses in which he poured brandy. Jacob Young's eyes shone.

'Sometimes you need it,' he exclaimed, handing glasses to his staff.

'Cheers.'

After taking two swigs, he continued.

'On the night of 20-21 October, what you know is happening. The caretaker of the library, Vernon Doyle, is brutally murdered in the church and his body found near the altar the next morning. And here is the second oddity: the doors are locked from the inside and there are no signs of forced entry. I have made two inspections and I am sure that there are no other exits, visible or hidden. Yet the killer managed to escape. Next to the body I found a small crucifix stained with blood, a fragment of gold depicting the Greek letter 'Ω' and soil that, with certainty, does not belong to the one in the garden in front, as it is lighter in colour, almost reddish, and of different consistency. Moreover, in the sacristy, near the corridor connecting the church to the library, there was an upturned chair and a kerosene lamp shattered; in the library, finally, I found this strange grassy substance on a shelf and, on the ground, Gordon found an empty chalice'.

The inspector took out of the drawer a sachet with the residue of the substance and one with the small fragment of gold, as well as the wooden chalice, which he left on the desk so that the officers could get an idea of it, then continued its reconstruction.

'At the moment the most credible dynamic is this: it's the middle of the night, Dr Burlow puts time of death between 3:00 and 5:00, and Vernon Doyle is in the library, we don't know what to do. At some point, he spots the killer hiding somewhere waiting for him and runs away terrified. He's holding a kerosene lamp, which falls on the floor when he hits a chair in the sacristy. The candles in the church are all out, since I found them with the wicks still white. Vernon Doyle knows the rooms perfectly, which he has frequented since childhood, and manages to reach the altar, where he stops and turns. He is then joined by the murderer, who is holding a knife with a blade at least half an inch thick, perhaps a hunting model; he approaches him and inflicts a first blow on his throat, which will reveal the deadly one. When you are attacked with a white weapon and have nothing to defend yourself with, you instinctively carry your hands forward as a form of protection. On his palms, however, I found nothing but superficial cuts that he caused himself by clutching the gold crucifix he always wore around his neck, so we must assume that Vernon Doyle did not see him leave. While he is dying on the ground the murderer positions himself above him, bends over his knees and strikes him twice more opening his stomach; the victim dies within seconds. The will to rage makes us understand that we are in the presence of an unscrupulous individual with clear symptoms of insanity.'

'How did the killer know he would have found Vernon Doyle at that time of night? Father Beathan told us he had plans to close the church around 8:30,' doubtful Gordon Craig asked.

'That's an excellent question, which I've been raving about from the very first moment. I'm sure once we find the answer, we'll find the killer.'

The inspector emptied the glass and filled it one more time, then left the bottle on the desk so that everyone was free to use it.

'Let's move on. In Inspector Morgan's office, as well as in the house, and let's move on to another very peculiar detail, I found nothing concerning the investigation into the disappearance of the manuscript. However, someone has taken the trouble to follow me there to spy on me...'

'Maybe it's the same person who attacked you,' interrupted Jacob Young, as if he had the most illuminating intuition.

'I exclude it with certainty; this afternoon, contrary to the doctor's instructions, I went out to check the footprints left by the attacker on the snow. Before he attacked me, I noticed that there were no tracks on the road, so whoever he was, had arrived through the woods. Well, they are different, smaller than those found outside Nevil Morgan's house, which most likely belonged to a man of large build. In fact, it is since my arrival in *Greystone* that I have the impression that I am being followed, and I am not usually mistaken about such things.'

'It's amazing how clues and traces create more questions than they can answer,' Craig said while the inspector stopped to give the two officers a voice.

'Every action has its own logic and every event has its own cause. By putting the pieces together, a coherent picture will emerge. We must be patient and analyse every detail, even the one that seems to us less important. We arrive at Vernon Doyle's funeral,' he continued, changing the subject, 'during the service someone, without being noticed, slipped this note into my pocket.'

He took a sheet of paper out of the desk drawer that he opened and laid out so that Gordon and Jacob could read its contents. It was written on it:

– I Invocation, II Apparition, III Imprisonment, IV Expulsion to the Underworld –

'Observe,' he said to the two agents, 'and tell me if you can grasp the meaning.'

Gordon Craig shook his head. Jacob Young seemed to be looking for a ghost hiding in the dark corners of his memory.

'I have a feeling I've heard this before,' he ventured, 'but I can't remember where or when.'

'Hopefully the antiquities expert I'm meeting tomorrow can tell us more. At the moment I preferred to keep this information to myself because it seems obvious that someone is trying to help us, but doesn't want to be identified, perhaps out of fear.'

The flame in the stove had become weaker and the inspector got up to add another large log of wood; then he went back to his seat.

'We need to find the author of this note, because he's probably aware of important information.'

'Where do we start?' Gordon Craig asked.

'Right now I am confused and still shaken by the aggression, but I ask you to think about it as soon as you get the chance. Study the handwriting well, it might come in handy.'

'Then there's Darrel Bennet,' Craig said again, 'what are we going to do about him?'

'Darrel Bennet is a prime suspect. There are too many coincidences that set him up, and while I have my doubts that he may have killed, we'll keep him here until we find out the real motive that led him to *Greystone.*'

'What about Adam Ford?' Jacob asked.

'Adam Ford's position also needs to be clarified. There is a heavy shadow hanging over him. The night of the murder, he was seen wandering through the woods between his house and the church. Even if the source doesn't have the greatest credibility, we have to believe it, until proven otherwise. I'd also like to know what relations link him to Judge Owen and Mayor Chapman, with whom he entered the library last night looking for something. I think I'll visit him again soon.'

Jacob Young was showing signs of fatigue. He seemed more clumsy than ever in his attempts to nip every yawn in the bud, but his flushed eyes spoke clearly.

'Now go and get some rest, you have every right to rest, and tomorrow take the morning off, as long as you calmly reflect on the situation and try to understand what it is that we're missing, especially you Jacob, who has been in *Greystone* the longest and know better the habits and peculiarities of this country.'

Upon hearing his name, Jacob Young gasped.

When the two policemen went out, Dorian Bayley was so tried that he could only consider what his most immediate needs were: to take a long rest and never abandon his revolver again.

28 October 1884 – Tuesday

'The master will see you in a moment.'
The housekeeper left a tray on the table and walked away discreetly. Dorian Bayley noticed the incredible variety of meticulously ordered books that decorated every wall in the room. In a corner near the fireplace two inlaid frames adorned ancient maps, while on a low three-legged table a display stand supported the remains of a stone slab engraved with geometric patterns.

'The globe of Babylon,' exclaimed a man who, in the meantime, had reached the inspector, 'is the oldest representation known today and dates back to the sixth century before Christ. As you will notice, Inspector, Babylon is located in the centre and is surrounded by the mythological Ocean River, while the triangles drawn on the outside represent islands and other emerged lands. It is a symbolic vision, of course, but it shows the passion with which some brilliant minds were animated by the desire for knowledge since ancient times. Look again,' added Edmund Vinson as he approached the wall on which the other two maps hung. He was an elegant man of small stature, between fifty and fifty-five, very thin, with short black hair and piercing dark eyes. A maniacally manicured upward moustache characterized him to such an extent that it would have been possible to recognize him in a crowd. He possessed a professorial manner and spoke in a calm but sure tone.

'This we can define as the birth of geography,' resumed pointing at the reproduction below, 'and represents the summary of the knowledge of Claudius Ptolemy, a famous

Egyptian astronomer and geographer. It dates back to the second century A.D., yet it shows what incredible precision was achieved in the calculation of space. Note especially the area of the Mediterranean, Africa and our continent. Here, finally,' he turned his attention to the second picture just above, 'I keep a copy of the famous *map mundi,* a theological vision of the world, but still an artistic masterpiece of the time. Its date is unknown, but it must have been drawn up between the 12th and 14th centuries A.D. Needless to add that we are in the presence of three copies, but perfect in every detail, worthy of being exhibited in a museum. I challenge any layman to certify their non-originality.'

Sir Edmund took his place on the sofa and invited his guest to do likewise. As soon as the inspector sat down, the antiquities expert poured the tea into two porcelain cups and handed him one, pointing to the sugar and milk container.

'Forgive me if I bore you, Inspector; sometimes I have a tendency to let myself go and I find I am too verbose.'

'On the contrary,' Dorian Bayley was able to take the floor, 'his brief lecture made me very curious and only confirms how well deserved your fame is.'

Edmund Vinson's eyes shone. He sipped tea while waiting for the inspector to tell him why he had asked for an appointment so urgently.

The head and shoulder pains were almost gone and that made Dorian Bayley free to think. Sir Edmund could have helped him untangle one of the last remaining tangled skeins in his head and allowed him to add a fundamental piece to the picture. As well as being a renowned auctioneer, in fact, Edmund Vinson was considered one of the greatest connoisseurs of ancient texts in the whole county. He found himself praising the research work of Jacob Young.

'Do you know an author named *Ambactus Danu*?'

Sir Edmund sighed, resting his back on the sofa, as he opened a silver door containing cigars and two pipes.

'Help yourself, Inspector,' he invited him while he carried a mahogany pipe in his mouth. 'This helps me think.'

Dorian Bayley took a cigar and carefully cut it. At the first generous mouthful, he appreciated its spicy aroma and exotic taste.

'As you have deduced yourself, Inspector, *Ambactus Danu* is not the real name of the author. We can consider him as such by convention, but given the different style used to write his work, it is likely that more people are hiding behind this enigmatic acronym.'

'More than one author?'

'No doubt; historically *Ambactus Danu* was the name of an ancient esoteric sect, born in England around the 15th century as a reaction to the nascent extremist politics of the Catholic Church, which was beginning to celebrate the first trials of the Holy Inquisition. *Danu* is the Celtic name of Dana, the universal mother goddess, while the *Ambactus* were her servants, or worshippers. Those who joined the sect, after a long initiatory journey, obtained the title of "worshipper and knight defender of the great Goddess Dana" and leaned towards a universal religious ideal based on the principle of a force that radiates every animate and inanimate being of the universe. Their thought of divinity resulted in something profoundly spiritual and non conceptualisable. In addition to this, the members of this sect looked with interest at various other pre-Christian mystics, all of them referring to a primordial naturalism, in which Mother Earth was the only recognized dogma; in a holistic vision of the universe, they were also refined connoisseurs of the mysterious alchemical disciplines and ancient magical arts, which they practiced almost always for good. The members of the *Ambactus Danu* considered themselves to be depositories of a knowledge handed down through generations, a knowledge aimed at maintaining the natural balance of things.'

'Almost always...' underlined Dorian Bayley, extrapolating the two words from context.

'Inspector, no matter how high an ideal may be, the danger remains that a corrupt mind may distort its original meaning and turn it into something very different.'

'Does this cult still exist?'

'Who knows,' Sir Edmund replied after finishing his tea, 'practicing magic arts or pursuing knowledge that contrasts with official belief can be very dangerous.'

'What do you think?'

'Such beliefs were born at the dawn of our history. To think that they can be extinguished I consider it at least a gamble. Are you asking me if such a cult can still be alive and operating? I'd say it's possible. I don't see why not... I don't see why not.'

'What do you know about the *Ambactus Danu* manuscript?'

Sir Edmund poured the inspector a second cup of tea, then did the same with his own.

'If you're talking about any one in particular, I'll tell you that it's worth nothing, neither magic nor cheap.'

Dorian Bayley was surprised and he gouged his eyes out. He didn't expect such a response but, in his mind, it was like putting a tiny missing gear in place that could set the whole mechanism in motion.

'You mean there are more copies?'

'On the contrary,' he hastened to point out the professor, inspiring the dull pipe. 'There is only one copy of the manuscript in the world, but it is part of a series of four books. If you want to know its economic value, no one will answer, if evaluated separately; the entire collection, on the contrary, is priceless.'

'Do you know its contents?'

'In the past I've tried to study it further, although I've never been able to access the originals. For this reason my knowledge may prove incomplete. The four manuscripts contain a series of rituals that would be able to defeat dangerous demonic entities. The peculiarity is that they are dependent on each other. Practically every single manuscript contains only a part of the ritual and, taken in its singularity, there is no effect, on the contrary, it could trigger harmful events. In the case of community celebration, on the contrary, following the correct time sequence and only after a deep preparation, they can become a formidable magical instrument. The idea of transcribing an esoteric formula by dividing it into four non-independent texts was probably due to the authors' desire to prevent a single man from centralizing such a frightening power in his own hands. In fact, no one has ever owned all four books at once. Many have tried, of course, but they have always found exceptional resistance on the part of their owners, who are more interested in safeguarding the beliefs and dogmas contained in them than in their potential economic value.'

'Do you know the titles of the four manuscripts?'

'Certainly,' Edmund Vinson replied, 'even though, to be honest, the books have no real titles; whoever wrote them merely classified them. For the sake of precision,' he added, taking a sheet of paper and an inkwell, 'I'll bring them back to you below, so that you can remember them in the future. At the moment I don't know who the owners are.'

'Do you believe in their esoteric power?' asked Dorian Bayley as he folded the paper and slipped it into the inside pocket of his coat. What he saw while taking the paper in his hand startled him, but he preferred to postpone the matter until later.

Sir Edmund did not seem surprised by the question; he put one hand into the rack and with two fingers grabbed a pinch of tobacco, which he methodically placed in the pipe stove; finally he turned it on and calmly inspired the sweetish aroma, which quickly spread through the room.

'Inspector, I have devoted myself to the study of ancient manuscripts since I was thirteen. I can say I'm an expert in almost all the disciplines of the humanities. This passion, however, has never prevented me from embracing one at all. I am fascinated by the study of magic and spiritualism and I am convinced that science can be a useful tool to understand the dynamics behind them. My experience as a scholar suggests to me that such phenomena must be understood and respected, since our society is still far from being able to give definitive answers to questions that we have been asking ourselves for centuries, if not millennia.'

'Sir Edmund, thank you for seeing me. You have been very helpful to my investigation.'

'I am grateful to you for giving me the opportunity to entertain such a stimulating discussion. Don't hesitate to come back if you still need it.'

As he stepped out of the gate, Dorian Bayley beckoned a coachman to approach. He took his place inside the car and closed the door, waiting for the coachman to take the road to *Greystone*. At the last moment, however, he decided to change destination; before returning to the police station he wanted to meet Madame Eleanor who, he was sure, must have known more than she had intended the first time.

He took the mysterious, authorless note, which someone had slipped into his pocket at Vernon Doyle's funeral and, compared it with what Sir Edmund had written. They both had the same words on them:

I) Invocation
II) Appearance
III) Imprisonment
VI) Expulsion to the underworld.

***

'Opportunity, means and motive,' thought Dorian Bayley as he was being thrown around because of the rough road reduced, in some places, to a potato field. He began to regret having preferred the carriage to the train, even though the beautiful snowy countryside reconciled him with the world. Had it not been for the annoying squeaking of the uneven wheels, he would have enjoyed a few hours of total peace of mind.

The discovery just made closed the circle of his suspicions. Adam Ford had lied several times; the value of the manuscripts, the presence in town of Darrel Bennet, the theft and disappearance of Inspector Morgan drew a coherent picture, where each piece seemed to fit perfectly. The art dealer had come to *Greystone* on commission from Sir Donald Acton, who intended to purchase the entire *Ambactus Danu* collection. Given the stakes, the well-known collector had given Darrel Bennet carte blanche, both on the amount of money he would have to pay and on how to acquire the precious manuscripts. In his opinion, Darrell Bennet had contacted Vernon Doyle, who considered him suitable after having taken information; when he learned that it was impossible to open normal negotiations with the owners of the books, however, the merchant had persuaded him to steal them on commission. There was no longer any doubt that the theft in the Fords' house was signed by Vernon Doyle himself. The position of Nevil Morgan remained to be clarified; Dorian Bayley did not rule out that a rich reward and the possibility of getting his hands on the four manuscripts had convinced the inspector to be part of the plan. His penchant for spiritualism may have been a key psychological lever to convince him to break the law. In the whole affair, it should not be forgotten that Darrel Bennet saw in the collection only an economic investment, not being a supporter of either spiritualism or magic, practices he did not believe in and did not give any credit to. Adam Ford, however, discovered the perpetrator of the theft, in an attempt to return to possession and being able to act undisturbed at night armed with a hunting knife, had first killed Vernon Doyle, perhaps at the height of a fight, and then Inspector Morgan, guilty of having put himself on his trail and certain that he would not allow to cover up a murder case without betraying his nature as a man of law. At this point Darrel Bennet, who had learned of the first murder, had fled to *Little Castle* under the pretext of the auctions held that week, so as to create an alibi for when he would return to *Greystone,* with the hope, remained alive, to get his hands on the collection. Though he would never endorse a murder, there was too much desire to complete a deal that would secure him a significant gain, perhaps more than he could have imagined. Having been unable to retrieve the book immediately after Vernon Doyle's murder, Adam Ford, helped in this by Judge Owen and Mayor Chapman, his accomplices or simply his friends, had finally returned to the library at night. It was likely that the search had not had the desired effect, since Dorian Bayley had previously thoroughly searched the rooms without finding any matches; unless, he thought, the book had been hidden using the simplest of systems: placing it in one of the shelves, confusing it with the others and passing it off as a simple searchable book. The investigations, however, had brought to light too many mistakes made, causing the alibis to be dismantled and the facts, crossed with each other, to lose coherence and credibility. Adam Ford had to know who the owners of the other manuscripts were and this exposed them to great danger, because the cemetery attendant had already shown that he had no scruples about eliminating anyone who could discover the truth and report everything to the police. Dorian Bayley knew that once the taboo that prevents a man from taking his own life was broken, the possibility of a relapse became more than likely. Dr Burlow also agreed with this theory when he talked about "mission accomplished".

In this perspective, the almost certain murder of Nevil Morgan became a simple incidental consequence. As much as he felt he had sufficient elements in his hands to close the case and as much as he knew the danger of keeping Adam Ford at large, Dorian Bayley decided not to proceed with any arrest. To consider the investigation complete, he first had to clarify the position of all the suspects and the weight each of them had had in the case. Immediately after visiting Madame Eleanor, he would rush to the police station to inform his agents of the developments of which he had become aware and ensure that the main suspects were followed day and night.

Shortly before arriving at *Greystone,* he carefully checked that the revolver was loaded. He asked the coachman to leave it on the edge of the woods, at the point where the path leading to Madame Eleonor's property began. He celebrated the usual ritual, lifting his lapel and putting his hands into the deep pockets of his coat, then he walked at a fast pace until the sun's rays stopped filtering through the vegetation which, from that moment on, became as thick as a pile of intertwined ropes.

After about thirty minutes he found himself in the bare clearing; he felt his feet frozen because of the cold and compact snow. He continued along the path until he saw a more intense light shattering on the trunks of the trees. He realized he had reached his destination. Silence reigned all around, even though the smoking chimney was proof that someone was in the house. When he knocked, a young woman he had never seen before opened the door. She greeted him with a slight bow and made him sit down in the kitchen. A sheet fixed on the doors where the door was missing, divided the ground floor into two rooms, making the small space in front of the entrance gloomy.

'I'd like to speak to Madame Eleonor,' said Dorian Bayley, addressing the girl as he approached a chair.

'The lady is busy at the moment; as soon as she's finished she'll be glad to talk to you.'

'If I may ask, madam, what kind of session are you celebrating?'

The girl hurried to ajar the door.

'Madame Eleonor received a visit from the Simmons couple and is trying to get in touch with their son Markus, who died six months ago from an illness the doctors were unable to cure.'

The inspector felt an arrow through his heart, but managed not to give in to the sadness, and was able to wake up with a jolt of the head.

'Does that mean he's practicing a séance?' he asked astonished.

'She prefers to call these experiences a conversation with souls,' replied the young woman with a sweet smile.

Waiting for the end of the session, he went out into the garden and lit a cigar. He lifted his head, half-closed his eyes and let himself be lulled by the placid noises of nature and intoxicated by its smells. At that moment, he felt a pleasant sensation of peace and it seemed to him that all the ugliness he was forced to live with every day because of his work had suddenly been swept away by the perfection of the forms he observed, daughters of a nature that could only give beauty. He was surprised to feel in a strange harmony with those who, in the past, had become members of the *Ambactus Danu* sect, with those who imagined the universe pervaded by a simple immanent, immobile, silent essence, and with those who aspired to a life in constant search of spiritual elevation, good and justice. In those moments the mind gave him back, vivid and intense, distant memories, jealously guarded in the deepest part of his being, from which he drew the energy necessary to move forward and not to give up in the face of a destiny that had too often shown him only the dark side of life. He became melancholy; he took a few steps, then knelt down and gathered snow on the palm of his hand, carrying it under his nostrils; he felt its purity. He was brought back to reality by the voice of the girl who was calling him.

'Inspector, come in.'

A whiff of cold air hit him in the back, giving him a long shiver.

'It was an emotion we'll never forget,' said a woman with a long scarf wrapped around her head, 'thank you very much.'

Madame Eleanor took her hands, smiling with her eyes shining from her emotion. The man next to her stood in silence with an incredulous face.

'Come back and see me anytime.'

The couple left the house and seemed to have regained their lost hope. Perhaps, thought Dorian Bayley, the psychological help that woman provided was really able to soothe the pain and that sense of bewilderment caused by loss.

'I'm glad to see you again, Inspector,' Madame Eleanor welcomed him and begged him to sit down.

'I'm sorry to bother you, but I already mentioned we'd see each other again. I need to know what you and Inspector Morgan said to each other the last time you saw each other. I have reason to believe he was in a bad situation.'

The woman did not bat an eye; she took a candle, placed it in the middle of the table and lit it, while her assistant stood in a corner near the window. She sat down and gathered her hands around a necklace.

'Inspector Nevil Morgan was very concerned. He told me about it the day before he disappeared. He was taking care of an investigation but I think his concern depended on something else.'

'Did he tell you what was troubling him?'

'His concern had deep roots. He asked me to help him so that the mere theft of a book wouldn't turn into something much more dramatic.'

'I don't think I'm following you,' remarked Dorian Bayley dazed. 'Does what you tell me have anything to do with the magic formulas in the manuscript?'

'Inspector, there is a terrible power shaking the bowels of the earth; the occurrence of exceptional conditions have allowed it to cross the threshold that keeps our world distinct from that of darkness. We must make sure that

evil is rejected and not allowed to bring more death among us.'
'More death? Does that mean it's already here?'
'All the clues confirm it. A greedy and weak man has allowed it to manifest itself, and now it is only a matter of time before it returns to show its blind ferocity.'
'Is this about Vernon Doyle, the librarian?' the inspector asked, raising his voice.
Suddenly, Madame Eleanor gouged out her eyes; she stiffened, tightening the edge of the table with the bony fingers of her hands. Her mouth contorted itself in a grotesque pose; her head fell backwards, her eyes becoming two white balls.
'Don't move, Inspector,' the assistant intervened and put her hands on her shoulders to support her.
'Are you feeling sick?'
The girl checked the seer's face, then turned to the inspector.
'She's gone into a trance. She's having a vision.'
The table started shaking and jerking like it was at the mercy of an earthquake. A window sash opened wide, bumping against the wall and a gust of wind blew out the candle. The curtain began to flutter as if it had been shaken by someone. Dorian Bayley watched in confusion; at any other moment he would have limited himself to understanding where were the artifices that allowed that staging but, in those moments, he felt inclined to doubt the reality in front of him and to believe that perhaps, beyond the physical laws, he was living and pulsating a shapeless universe able to regulate life with different laws.
When the wind died down and Madame Eleanor recovered, Dorian Bayley felt enveloped by an aura of mysticism. He wanted to believe that the woman was acting in good faith.

'Evil is among us,' the seer began, speaking with difficulty, 'before it can be stopped, it will strike again. If you want this story to end, Inspector, agree to go beyond your beliefs.'

'What do you mean he's going to strike again? Madame Eleanor, if you know where Inspector Morgan is, you'd better tell me now.'

'The inspector is no longer with us, but has just appeared to me in a vision; his body is in a dark and cold place, hidden from men's sight.'

In saying those words, the woman fainted. This time, however, her body appeared relaxed and her face fell forward and leaned against her chest. Her breathing was regular.

'Madame Eleanor must rest, Inspector, let's leave her alone,' sentenced the assistant as if she were used to that sequence of events.

She took a blanket and laid it on her shoulders.

Dorian Bayley followed the girl outside the house and together they reached the edge of the property.

'Do you work here?' the inspector asked.

The girl could be 25 years old at most; despite the simple dress she was wearing, her features were elegant and very attenuated. Her rosy face was highlighted by long blonde hair, which made the emerald colour of her eyes stand out.

'I visit her two or three times a week; I help her with household chores and try to make myself useful when she receives people in need of her help.'

'May I know your name?'

The girl bent her head and blushed her face. She started rubbing her sweaty hands on her dress.

'My name is Sandra.'

'Thank you Sandra, now go and see if Madame Eleanor is feeling better.'

***

From the moment he left the house, Dorian Bayley had done nothing but think about his son. That indissoluble shadow that enveloped his days with a constancy similar to an eternal fog could turn, as in that moment, into a deafening thunderstorm. To find shelter in those moments it was necessary to project oneself into another dimension without time, without space and without memories.

He focused on the sound of his footsteps, waiting for the thought to turn elsewhere. It happened so, without any warning, freeing him from a pain that bit him in the neck like a mad dog, taking his breath away.

To free him from that grip were the voices of children, which increased in intensity as he approached the police station along Main Street. When he arrived at the intersection, he did not turn towards the police station, but went in the opposite direction; it was from there that the festive screams came. He walked about a hundred steps and found himself facing the entrance gate to the house of Mayor Nickolas Chapman, preceded by a large garden, an expanse of well-kept green grass, where a crowd of children were jumping and running, watched by a group of adults talking to each other.

Dorian Bayley stopped near the open gate to observe and at first no one noticed his presence. A man dressed in an elegant dark coat and shiny leather shoes broke away from the group of adults and drew the attention of the children aloud.

'As every year, dear children, we are ready to start the treasure hunt in honour of the harvest season which, this year too, is giving so much satisfaction to the inhabitants of this magnificent place. As you well know, we have scattered clues for the village and some of the inhabitants, our accomplices, will be able to give you valuable information so that you can find the hidden treasure and thus win the title of winners.'

There arose cries of excitement from the little ones.

'But like any self-respecting treasure hunt,' continued the mayor, striving to speak solemnly, 'we have chosen an exceptional godmother to conduct the couples' draw, provide the clue to the start and reward the participants.

The mayor looked towards the group of adults and nodded to a woman to approach. It was a very young girl, in her twenties. She was quite slender and did not seem at all excited or intimidated by the presence of the mayor and the other spectators.

'Here she is in all her beauty,' said the mayor in a ceremonial voice, paying tribute to the girl with a blatant bow. 'We have the honour to have with us Godmother Sarah Benson.'

A composed applause resounded in the air.

'Sarah Benson,' thought astonished Dorian Bayley.

That name was not new to him; though he could not remember on what occasion, he was certain that he had heard it before. He didn't even have time to tidy up his thoughts and noticed that the mayor had noticed his presence and, while the girl had begun to speak explaining the rules of the game, he was giving him flashy hand signals inviting him to come in and join the company.

The inspector approached the mayor, who turned to him in a low voice so as not to disturb the presentation.

'At last, Inspector Bayley, I'm delighted to make your acquaintance. As a representative of the people of

Greystone, I want to express our gratitude for what you're doing.'

Dorian Bayley was surprised by the mayor's good-natured attitude; for no apparent reason, in the past few days, he had imagined him to be shy and not very good-natured.

'Thank you, Mr Mayor, I hope to shed light on the terrible events in the village as soon as possible and allow the inhabitants to appreciate as before the wonders this place has to offer.'

The mayor nodded his head in gratitude and, together, they continued to follow the ceremony.

When Sarah finished speaking, the children's couples set up just outside the gate waiting to go. They were all very excited and looking forward to their adventure.

Recent events had suggested a variant in the draw. The couples had to be made up of one older and one younger child, so the names were drawn from two different ballot boxes. Among the adults present, some would search the area where the game would develop, ensuring the safety of the children and the peace of mind of their parents who, in the meantime, would entertain themselves in the mayor's garden, where some tables had been prepared on which two maids served hot tea and pastries.

Mayor Chapman had begged Dorian Bayley to stay until the award ceremony. The inspector realised he had become a prominent figure in *Greystone* and did not feel like backing out. Some of the parents present came forward and introduced themselves. Dorian Bayley noticed with curiosity that his name was known even to those he had never seen before.

Among the volunteers was Martin Ford. He saw him sipping a cup of tea while he was arguing with a friend of his that the inspector had already seen in the main square

of the village. He went to the table, was served a cup of tea with biscuits, and he approached.
'Today the sun has given us his mercy,' he said to the cemetery caretaker's son.
Martin turned and drew a grimace of amazement on his face.
'Inspector Bayley, I'm glad to see you again. Are you around here too?'
'I happened to be passing by and I heard some rumours; in my line of work one must be curious.'
'I'm sorry I can't entertain you, but I'm here to take the children on the treasure hunt. This is an event that the community organizes every year and the children care about it very much; however, recent events have brought a lot of mistrust in the village and this year it was decided not to let them go alone.'
'I guess,' nodded the inspector.
'Oh, but how careless,' resumed Martin Ford pointing to his friend, 'this is Deven Bell, my childhood friend; together we decided to dedicate a couple of hours of our time to allow this beautiful initiative to succeed. His younger brother is among the participants in the game and that's why he suggested I come here.'
Deven was tall and thin. He had red hair, freckles and a clumsy look. He waved goodbye with his head, almost intimidated by the presence of the police officer and immediately lowered his gaze.
Dorian Bayley said goodbye in return, then gave way to the two who headed for the gate and disappeared along with the group of escorts and children who were starting their treasure hunt.
Left alone, he was sure that Martin was Adam Ford's adopted son. There was not only an excessive age difference with his mother; confirming his suspicions was

the absolute lack of similarity with both parents. Martin was a tall, strong boy with a pronounced jaw and thick black hair. The Fords were both thin and not very tall, with a round face and a completely different expression.

He put the matter of Martin Ford aside and took his notebook out of his pocket. He scrolled through the pages of notes taken the night he met George Davies, until he found Sarah Benson's name.

'She is the little girl who was lost in the woods fifteen years ago,' he thought surprised, 'and who, it is said, was found thanks to a vision of Madame Eleanor.'

After not even five minutes, Dorian Bayley was sipping a cup of tea sitting next to the girl. She said she was fascinated by London and promised to take a trip there soon. Although dressed in plain clothes and the daughter of artisans, Sarah Benson possessed good oratory skills. The inspector judged that she must have come from an educated family and that, over the years, she had devoted herself to study, something not common among village girls. She could modulate her tone of voice with discretion, and the almost complete lack of dialectal inflection was proof that good English was heard in the family. She liked to talk, that was clear, and Dorian Bayley took the plunge to slide the conversation into what had happened 15 years earlier.

'I was a little girl and I had already had a great desire to explore,' she said. 'One Sunday morning I had looked out the door while my parents were busy with chores and preparations for lunch. I thought I saw a huge black shadow at the end of the alley, along the path that wedges into the woods. I still feel like I'm seeing the scene through the eyes of a five-year-old girl. I was frightened but, intrigued, I decided to go and see it. I walked along the path until I saw footprints on the ground that were lost in the woods; I followed them without hesitation. The footprints often changed direction so I was disorientated. Terrified, I realized I was lost. I thought about following the footprints backwards, but I couldn't find them either, as if the ground had reabsorbed them. I had wandered far away and didn't know which direction to go home in. I started to scream, but soon, the fear was so strong that it suffocated my screams in my throat. I can still feel that fear over me. So vivid that when I think about it, I get the shivers. I tried to shout "Mummy" but, no matter how hard I tried, I couldn't get anything out but a flickering thread of voice. I can't remember how long I wandered in the woods. I ran without a precise destination, looking for a path, a tree, a known bush that could orient me. But everywhere I turned I saw only vegetation. I fell several times, hurting my legs and face.'

'It must have been terrible,' consoled Dorian Bayley.

'At a certain point I stopped; my breath began to subside and in a moment I was no longer afraid. I felt a conviction taking hold of me. Someone would soon come for me. I was so convinced that I even stopped crying. I found a boulder and sat on it; my mother had taught me how to count with my fingers, so I started counting with ten fingers and then started again and so on. I thought that from that day on my lucky number would be the one I would call a moment before I saw the person who would save me; the fear and anguish had suddenly vanished, and I had not even half a doubt that I would soon return home. When the silhouette of Edward Lambert in uniform appeared from behind a tree, the number four on my hand was in my vision.

'Four must be a very important number around here,' exclaimed Sibylline Dorian Bayley.

The girl didn't get the reference and went on.

'Later they told me that it was Madame Eleanor who told the police the exact place to look for me. It was as if in those moments we had made contact; inside me I could hear her calm voice asking me to wait there and not to move. Over the years, I have given this explanation for what happened, it couldn't be otherwise. My family and I will be eternally grateful to Madame Eleanor for what she has done for us. My sister often comes to her to assist her during her sessions without asking for anything in return because, she says, the greatest reward is to see the eyes of those to whom good is done.'

'What's your sister's name?' asked the inspector who actually knew the answer.

'Sandra Benson, she's my older sister.'

Dorian Bayley mentioned a smile but said nothing about what he had seen at Madame Eleanor's house.

The girl's face had changed as she recounted her adventure; it was like reliving those terrible moments, from the surprise of seeing the shadow of a large animal wandering through the dark alleys of the village to the joy of liberation from her little nightmare. It seemed that in the village everything revolved around the same beliefs, in a symbolic circuit that recalled the titles of the four manuscripts: invocation, apparition, imprisonment, cast into hell.

The walls, the trees and the inhabitants' souls were impregnated with that symbolism, in a waltz of ambiguity that continually brought us back to our starting point.

Dorian Bayley realized the real risk of falling into the game of secular beliefs that obscured the power of reason, and was convinced that this would be an insurmountable obstacle in the search for truth. He strove to remove any form of thought that deviated from all that was demonstrable, possible and provable. He related Sarah

Benson's story to a frightening adventure with a happy ending that the fantasies of a little girl and a superstitious community prone to easy supernatural explanations had elevated to a spiritual event.

***

By the time Adam Ford got home it was 6:00 p.m. and it was already pitch black in *Greystone.* On the lane leading to his house some oil lamps hadn't been recharged and Jacob Young thought it was a real fortune. He had been instructed never to let the cemetery attendant out of his sight and he had taken this very seriously, regardless of the fact that his shift would soon be over. Dorian Bayley had revealed to him that there was a good vantage point at the back of the house where he could listen to conversations coming from inside, especially when the darkness of the evening became a faithful ally.
To avoid catching another cold, this time Jacob wore two warm wool sweaters, heavy trousers and knee-length socks, covered with sturdy ankle boots with high leather soles. A long coat, with gloves, hat and scarf, guaranteed him adequate protection against the cold that, in the last tail, had proved to be the most insidious enemy.
He waited for Adam Ford to enter the house and then, with quick steps, sneaked into the garden around the building on the right to head to the back. The lack of light did not allow him to notice a pile of scrap metal piled up on one wall of the house and the officer crashed into it, falling to the ground in an annoying roar. He hurt his knee and made an effort not to curse out loud while praying that the noise would not attract the attention of those in the house. He stood still for a minute and then breathed a sigh of relief; no one came to check. He breathed a sigh of

relief and reached the window that the inspector had pointed out to him. He found it closed, but a small tug was enough to open it as much as he needed to eavesdrop. The condensation had fogged up the glass and this allowed him to keep a short distance without being seen. The room he was looking out the window was dark and Jacob sensed it must have been a small study. Not even time to become familiar with the situation, he saw a flickering light approaching and a large shadow projected in a multiform way on the walls. He snapped back and cornered himself. A man had entered the closet with a lamp in his hand and walked right towards him.

'This time he caught me,' he thought terrified.

He saw a hand go out the window, grab the handle and pull it inwards, making it return to the position where the officer had found it.

'Did anyone ask George Davies when he could come and fix this handle?' shouted Adam Ford in an irritated tone as he left the room.

A male and a female voice gave a negative answer.

'If this keeps up, I'm going to die of a heart attack,' Jacob Young thought.

A few minutes later, the full Fords came down for dinner. The dining room was adjacent to the little room, and this gave the officer a clear understanding of what was being said.

'It was fun,' Martin Ford was saying, referring to the early afternoon treasure hunt, 'the children were enthusiastic and it was a good opportunity for adults to exchange a few words. You should have seen the look on Deven Bell's face when he heard that it was his little brother who won the winner's prize; he was pretending to be aloof but he was close to screaming and jumping for joy.'

'Of course,' noted the mother, 'it's strange how two brothers are the perfect opposite. The little one is active, shrewd, almost cheeky. Deven, on the other hand, is shy, always ready to apologize for existing in the world.'

Adam Ford gave off a muffled grin from the food he was still chewing.

'I'd say more than shy,' Martin continued, 'when he saw Inspector Bayley arrive he almost sank into the ground in shame.'

'What was the inspector doing in Mayor Chapman's backyard?' Adam Ford interrupted.

'I think he just happened to drop by and the mayor invited him in.'

'Sure,' said Adam Ford sarcastically. 'He just happened to pass by...'

'I think so,' replied his son, 'and besides, he's staying a stone's throw from Mayor Chapman's house, and I don't see what would be wrong with that.'

'This trusting Inspector Bayley denotes great naivety on your part,' rebuked his father.

For a couple of minutes all you could hear was the sound of cutlery rubbing against the crockery, then Martin resumed.

'I think the best thing would be to tell the inspector the truth. There's no point in going into hiding.'

'Once again you're proving to be naive, Martin.'

Adam Ford took a break, then the sound of a glass being violently placed on the table was heard.

'Do you understand that if I tell the inspector the truth, it will be the end of me, or rather,' he paused a little while longer, 'the end of us?'

'I think you're overreacting, Dad. If the inspector could understand why you're acting the way you are, maybe he could help you.'

Adam Ford raised his voice.

'Inspector Bayley, if you remember correctly, has already been here. Without too much ado, he implied that he would take great pleasure in seeing me in prison. Do you really want me to give him a good excuse to arrest me? Remember, it's not just my life at stake, it's a lot of other people's.'

No one responded.

'It would be better to continue this conversation tomorrow morning,' his mother intervened, 'now you will be tired and nervous, you will see that as soon as you wake up you will find a point of agreement.'

'I'd say it would be better not to continue this conversation tomorrow or ever,' Adam Ford closed the conversation.

Jacob would have wanted to run to the inn where Dorian Bayley was staying to report what he had heard, but he managed to hold his frenzy and remain lucid. He decided that, until the Fords went to sleep, he would stay lurking around and get as much information as he could. He was very excited to feel an active part of a murder investigation, he who until ten days earlier had limited himself to breaking up a few brawls in the pub or collecting complaints about nocturnal noise. When dinner was over, however, the family retired to the upper floor. Together with the darkness fell a deep silence, suddenly interrupted by a small animal that quickly crossed the brambles, making the officer jump.

Jacob Young was satisfied with the work he had done. As he left the Fords' house, this time he was careful not to make the slightest noise. The next morning, he would go to the police station and report to the inspector. He felt that this time he would do a great service not only to the investigation, but also to the people of *Greystone* who, thanks to his stubbornness, would understand who the evil was using to stretch his slimy tentacles.

31 October 1750

When the torch fire began to ignite the shrubs that bordered the base of the hearth, a blaze suddenly burst out, releasing a yellowish flame streaked with deep black ribbing. The darkness was ripped open like a canvas by a knife. The primordial dance of fire began to cast restless shadows on the rock walls, drawing winged figures and grotesque abstract shapes.

'Burn and purify,' pronounced a voice with a cavernous timbre, the echo of which dispersed into the most hidden recesses of the chamber, flooding the environment like a dense liquid.

On the sides of an imaginary square surrounding the fireplace were drawn four circles containing four triangles, each lit by three candles placed at the vertices. Outside the square, one next to the other, four men stood still waiting for a higher order. They were dressed in a dark tunic closed at the waist by a rope and had their faces painted with natural pigments, veiled under a wide hood as if they were prisoners of the night. In their right hand the Grand Masters held a manuscript, in their left hand a parchment in which part of an ancient magic ritual had been transcribed, whose origins were lost in the shapeless folds of time.

Silence created an ideal bridge to transport minds into the ancestral dimension from which everything had originated, where time and space lost their natural supports and where the infinite circular movement cyclically brought the world of the living and the dead together. In those moments, the powerful inertial forces allowed the doors to open, creating a passage capable of destabilizing the equilibrium of the entire universe. It was the task of the Grand Masters of *Ambactus Danu* to ensure that the founding pillars would not collapse under the weight of primordial chaos, from whose defeat the natural order of things was born in the unchanging time of myth.

The ferrous smell of the earth mixed with the constant humidity in the cave, making the air dense and difficult to breathe.

'Burn and purify,' was heard rumbling in the circular room.

'Burn and purify,' sang together like a funeral litany.

The fire seemed to respond to that invocation, roaring and rising as if a force was stirring ferociously from within.

The next silence was interrupted by the slight sound of footsteps approaching; from the darkness of a side ravine slowly took shape the vague contours of a woman. She approached the hearth firmly and swayed her hands, drawing sinuous shapes in the air. The flame turned blue and began to repeat its movements as if hypnotized. Madame Althea whispered something incomprehensible, then increased the timbre of her voice. The movements of the body became convulsive and a liberating scream, followed by a violent movement of the arms, which soar into the air and fall violently on the ground, made the flame explode, which split into many small flames that began to float on the vault of the chamber as if they were weightless.

The destiny of men crossed the battle against the evil that was advancing to cross the threshold. Before the day dawned, only one between light and eternal darkness would impose its dominion, redrawing the plots of the universe and pushing it toward a destiny which, if it had not seen its ancient balance shine forth, would have plunged without appeal into the flames of primordial chaos.

29 October 1884 – Wednesday

'Good morning, Inspector Bayley, to what do I owe the pleasure of this new visit?'
Adam Ford's face was worth a thousand words. Nervous and upset by that morning surprise, he did nothing to hide it. He was on his way out to the cemetery to do some routine work and did not intend to give much time to the pungent questions that the inspector would soon ask him.
A little less than an hour earlier, around seven o'clock, Dorian Bayley was walking back and forth in his inn room, undecided whether to go down to the breakfast room that was opening at that hour, or to wait behind the window to look for an idea, an intuition that might add something to the strange path he had travelled so far.
Someone knocked on the door and it seemed to him that he was afraid of being heard, so weak had been the blows. He went to open the door and was confronted by Jacob Young.
Aware that the information he had received the night before would have increased Dorian Bayley's esteem for him, the young officer had told the story in one breath, omitting the episode of the fall to the ground, a detail that could have blown up the stakeout.
What he received in return was a pat on the shoulder and the assignment to continue Adam Ford's stalking with the same self-sacrifice.
'The circle is tightening,' the inspector urged him, 'more interesting things will come out.'

He asked him to lurk around the cemetery while he was visiting Adam Ford that morning, trying to catch him by surprise before he left the house to go to work.

'I just came to ask you a couple of questions, Mr Ford. I'll try not to disturb you for long.'

'Forgive me, Inspector, but I was just on my way to work.'

'Who are the owners of the other three books, Mr Ford?' the inspector asked, ignoring his words.

'What kind of question is that? I've just told you that I have little time and I can't stand here and be interrogated right now,' he protested.

'Would it be an interesting alternative to come down to the station and be detained until I can dispel all my doubts?'

Adam Ford realized that at that moment he had to succumb; however, he did not let the inspector sit in the house, but stood on the doorway with the face of someone who had just swallowed a handful of salt.

'I don't know what books you're talking about.'

'I again take the liberty of doubting your words.'

'These are just provocations I don't intend to follow up on.'

Adam Ford's face had turned red with rage.

At that moment his son Martin came out of the house; he waved to his father and bowed his head as he passed in front of the inspector, then, with a quick step, came out of the gate and turned right.

'Perhaps you are convinced that in all this time I have not found information about the theft of the manuscript? Do you really think I'm that naive?'

'I suffered the theft of a book and as it is done in these cases I have filed a regular complaint. That I can tell you, nothing more. I don't understand what other books you're talking about.'

'That's what you have already told me, Mr Ford,' said Dorian Bayley flaunting a certain impatience, 'but now I have proof that you are lying and once again I want to be honest with you; lying in a murder case is in itself a crime for which I could take you to court.'

The inspector was aware that the judge in question would be Frank Owen, with whom he had been caught entering the church in the company of Mayor Chapman in the middle of the night. However, he wanted to keep the cards hidden so as not to allow anyone involved with the disappearance of Nevil Morgan and the murder of Vernon Doyle to plan a plot to confirm his innocence.

Adam Ford muttered something the inspector couldn't understand. On his face, always serious and bordering on angry, he read for a moment confusion and a hint of fear.

'Believe me,' Bayley resumed in a much more friendly tone, 'there is nothing that cannot be confessed, especially when confession can put an end to a series of events that upset an entire village. We both know you want it in your heart as much as I do.'

He let a few seconds pass so that the message was internalized.

Dorian Bayley knew his job like nobody in the world. He had played with Adam Ford like a tyrant who, during a storm, closed the door of the house and left his wife on the doorway, in the rain and gusts of wind, only to go out and offer her a blanket and thus become a magnanimous benefactor. It was a trick he often used when he understood with absolute certainty that his interlocutor was lying. Then he would push mercilessly until he perceived on the other side a hesitation, a slight hint of fear. This meant that the game was over, and it was time to reach out to your rival and bring him to your side.

'Tonight, about seven o'clock, I'll visit you again, Mr Ford, and over a hot drink, you'll see that our talks will come to a common point of view.'

The graveyard keeper returned to the house. Dorian Bayley took the direction of the gate but, before leaving, he stopped to assess the footprints left by Martin Ford on a pile of dirt he had stepped on. Then he took his notebook, wrote a note and left the house.

***

Dorian Bayley felt it was right not to stand idly by and wait for Adam Ford's return. He decided to visit Father Beathan, with whom he would have liked to talk about matters that had been left unresolved for some time; no one more than the priest could tell him in detail who the inhabitants of *Greystone* were, what customs they had and what personalities attended the church and had relations with Inspector Morgan and Vernon Doyle. The question that had been buzzing in his head since the pathologist confirmed the time of the murder: why was Vernon Doyle in the church in the middle of the night?

The most logical answer is that he was trying to hide something, but someone must have followed him and, once he had killed him, had taken possession of the manuscript. If the book had been recovered, why did Adam Ford return to the library with Judge Owen and Mayor Chapman? And why kill with such brutality?

Unsure where to find Father Beathan, he started from the house and took the little road that wedged into the woods. When he arrived at the door, he knocked several times without getting an answer. He decided to look for him in the church, but he didn't have time to turn around and heard a noise coming from inside the house. He put his hand in his coat pocket and the contact with the cold iron of the gun gave him security.

'Hello?' He shouted unanswered this time as well.

The window on his left was just ajar and Dorian Bayley didn't think twice. He climbed over the windowsill trying not to make noise and found himself inside a small kitchen. The fire was out and the metal pots and pans were hanging immobile from a shelf attached to the wall. He went to the adjacent room, a living room used as a dining room. There was an extinguished fireplace on the left wall, while a bookcase with shelves almost entirely covered the opposite wall. He briefly reviewed the texts; for the most part they were religious treatises but there were also manuscripts by missionaries and travellers describing the life and customs of distant cultures; also books on Western philosophy, from the classics to the more modern ones. Next to the shelves appeared a shelf in which there were medallions engraved with religious symbols, a small empty stoup and a snow crampon. Dorian Bayley watched them while his right hand held firmly the gun he held inside his coat pocket. A second crampon was on the floor in the bedroom, where he found the bed made, a pair of slippers and some clothes carefully folded over a chair with a woven straw seat. On the bedside table there was an empty glass. Suddenly Dorian Bayley had a gasp: behind him he saw a shadow whizzing through the living room, heading towards the kitchen. He turned and glimpsed a cat's tail disappearing at full speed behind the side door pillar. He breathed a sigh of relief and trained his grip on the weapon. When he left the house he changed his mind about what to do. He thought he had been naive in ordering Jacob Young to inspect Vernon Doyle's house shortly after the murder. The officer hadn't reported anything specific to him, but the inspector felt it was important to pay him a second visit. What an untrained eye might not see could be significant to him. Before, however, he walked for a long time, touching every place that had had to do with the terrible events of which *Greystone* had been the scene. Near the church he met Gordon Craig, who had asked for a few hours off to run some errands.

'Good morning, Gordon,' the inspector greeted him, smiling. 'I'm looking for Father Beathan. Have you seen him?'

'I've been around for a while, Inspector, but I don't seem to have crossed paths with him,' replied the officer, hinting at a greeting.

'Are you obsessed with the mystery surrounding this church, too?' asked Dorian Bayley, who didn't expect to find the agent there.

The officer looked circumspect; at first he seemed surprised to see his superior, but then he replied with a smile.

'Who isn't here in town? Events of this magnitude can only be heard in the speeches of drunks at the Golden Pub, but in reality no one here has ever experienced them.'

'We'll get to the bottom of it, Gordon, I guarantee you.' The inspector cheered him up.

The two of them separated, agreeing to meet at the police station in the afternoon.

***

After searching Vernon Doyle's house from top to bottom, when he had resigned himself to leaving with a handful of flies in his hand, the inspector found something interesting. The bed was undone, with the blankets lying twisted and a pillow now deformed on one side. On a chair set under a small desk was a second pillow, covered with a pillowcase that still smelled of lavender. The inspector took it in his hand and began to feel it; to the touch he felt something rigid. He opened the pillowcase and took out a small note on which it was written:

– 3 30 – for the forest –

The inspector's mind ran straight to the night of the murder. The numbers most likely referred to a time, while the path that cut through the woods came close to the church. If he had discovered such a clue at once, he thought by re-reading the contents of the note, the investigation could have taken a precise direction from the beginning. On the other hand, if Vernon Doyle hadn't had the care to hide it, someone could have taken it before Jacob Young's inspection. It was likely that those who had followed him several times, often anticipating his intentions, had already been in that house to try to eliminate any compromising traces; on the other hand, the entrance door was badly damaged and easily violated, with the eroded wood just at the height of the pawl. To pick the lock, Dorian Bayley simply slipped the tip of a key into the space that had formed in the middle and pushed inwards; a matter of seconds.

The rest of the house was modest and dirty; in the old kitchen, bare and cold, scraps of spoiled food lay forgotten on an old dark wooden table. The nauseating smell had forced Dorian Bayley to keep a handkerchief on his nose for the duration of the inspection.

'A humble home for a humble person,' he thought, recalling the description the villagers had made of Vernon Doyle and the words spoken by Father Beathan at the funeral.

'An appointment,' he thought, rereading the card, 'it's a meeting, but with whom?'

It seemed obvious that the killer could have been the one who set him up at that hour. The question was whether this had asked him to meet him at the church or at an outside place and then convinced him to come in later. And that mysterious dilemma remained unsolved:
'How did he get out of the church after the murder?'
Then, suddenly, as if dragged by a wave, he stopped thinking about how and why. Inside the house he formulated the vivid image of a man. A melancholic and lonely man who for once in his life had dared to go beyond his own moral principles, committing a sin. On a cold autumn night, the man rolled relentlessly into his bed, messing it up and twisting the blankets, waiting for the appointed time to come. Then he had got up and braved the merciless cold and black darkness of the woods at night to meet his terrible fate.
Dorian Bayley felt so sorry for the man that he had to leave the house in such a hurry. He had to get that painful image that had appeared before him out of his mind, as if he had known Vernon Doyle all his life, as if he was able to intercept his saddest emotions and make them his own, even though he had never seen him even once.

***

The appointment with the officers had been set for the evening in the inspector's office. The main purpose was to clarify the position of Darrel Bennet, at the moment the only one formally accused of at least being involved with the theft of the manuscripts.
When the inspector returned to the police station it was still 5.30 p.m. and Father Beathan was waiting for him.
'Good evening, Inspector, I met Constable Craig and he said you wanted to talk to me.'

'Thank you, but you didn't need to bother coming all the way out here, father. I just wanted to ask you if there's anything new and if you've noticed anything strange lately among the people who regularly attend the church.'

'People are afraid, Inspector. And for that I don't feel like blaming anyone. They show a strong will to see the perpetrator of these hideous crimes, perpetrated with God knows what cruelty.'

'I understand,' said the inspector who, in the meantime, had seen Jacob Young approaching, 'I guarantee you that light will be shed on what happened in *Greystone* and that the people will be able to live peacefully again.'

'For my part, Inspector, I don't seem to have detected any strange behaviour lately. In my own little way, I try to convince men that even the most frightening fears can be overcome with the power of faith.'

Saying this, he reached his hands to his pelvis and bowed his head.

'Father,' Dorian Bayley took back as if to grasp a question that had been lost in the dark of his memory, 'do you think there's a reason why Vernon Doyle was in church in the middle of the night?'

Father Beathan spread his arms.

'Vernon was an introverted man, but as long as I've known him, he's never done anything weird like this. He lived from home and church, never went out at night and, as far as I know, not once did he set foot in an inn. He often confessed and listened to my words. He never did anything without warning me first and often needed my approval. Not that I wanted to manage his life, but his devotion to me was unconditional and he was happy like that.'

Dismissed Father Beathan, the inspector sent Officer Young to call Darrel Bennet.

The young policeman seemed uncomfortable. He took a few steps then turned back towards the inspector who looked at him intrigued.

'Around 3:00 in the afternoon I lost track of him,' he said in a fearful voice.

'You're talking about Adam Ford, right?'

Young bowed his head.

'I've been looking for him all afternoon but he seems to have vanished into thin air.'

Bayley reflected for a moment then decided that he would deal with the matter later.

'Now go get Bennet,' concluded.

Meanwhile Gordon Craig arrived and after a few minutes all four of them were sitting in the inspector's office.

'The time has come to tell the truth Mr Bennet,' attacked the inspector 'now that we are one step away from the solution, keeping silent for you will only prove to be a weapon contested in reverse.'

'I'm stunned, Inspector. You had the courage to keep an honest man like me in prison for days, a man who dedicated his life to knowledge, art and culture.'

Dorian Bayley turned to the two agents sitting at the side of the desk with an expression typical of who was sure that nothing would come out of that conversation. There were only two possibilities: either Bennet was a seasoned criminal to whom a few days in prison was not enough to make him spill his guts, or he was innocent and lived in the belief that his position would soon be clarified with an official apology from the police. Dorian Bayley, almost obsessed with logic and the belief that cause-effect relationships explained much more than chance and coincidence, believed Darrel Bennet was more involved than words and alibis told. Since his appearance in the village, there had been a succession of unusual events such as the theft of the manuscript, which, among other things, coincided with his interests as a collector and seller of antiques. He had disappeared as soon as Vernon Doyle was killed and fled from the sight of Gordon Craig at *Little Castle*. When a jigsaw puzzle fit so well Dorian Bayley rejected the idea that the pieces had been thrown up in the air and, as they hit the ground, they had stuck on their own. It was easier to believe that one or more people had committed themselves to putting the figure back together again, and to completing a project they'd been working on for some time.

He then decided to attack with his head down to check his interlocutor's reaction.

'You hired Vernon Doyle to steal the book from Adam Ford's house. But you hadn't come to terms with the man's personality. In fact, the library attendant immediately regretted what he'd done and blamed it all on Inspector Nevil Morgan. Then you killed both of them and then left the village resigned to the fact that there was no point in trying to recover the other three manuscripts with the dust that was rising.'

'I see you've taken information about the existence of the collection, Inspector.'

Bennet made a grimace that was hard to interpret.

'So you're confessing Mr Bennet?' Dorian Bayley jumped at it, though he was aware that in his impromptu reconstruction the issues that didn't add up were too many.

'I confess nothing Inspector,' Bennet shook his head firmly, 'I am an art expert and a collector of esoteric objects and books. That's why I know the legend of the *Ambactus Danu* sect and the texts they keep in great secrecy.'

'Mr Bennet, what does it feel like when you plunge a knife into a human being's body?'

The question point-blank left everyone present speechless. There was no time for a reply because the door to the room opened wide without anyone knocking. As if he was out of his mind, breathless and with a grainy look, Judge Owen entered.

'Run quickly, someone killed Margaret in my house and stole a manuscript,' he could say despite his breath.

The silence fell; a silence full of tension, fear, disappointment.

The two officers looked at each other and then sprang to their feet preparing to take orders from the inspector.

Dorian Bayley put on his coat and put the gun in his pocket.

'Agent Young, take the gentleman back to his cell and join us outside,' he said as he invited Craig to follow him with a wave of his hand.

As he left the room, the inspector turned back. He was looking for the look on Darrel Bennet's face, who, though, held his head down. His face was pale and sweaty, as if he were about to faint.

***

The accusations that Dorian Bayley had made against Darrel Bennet contained nothing but pure provocation unsupported by concrete evidence; the inspector was well aware of this. Bluffing was part of his job and he played it, as always, like a real professional. This time, however, it had gone wrong because the judge had entered with the terrible news that in fact exonerated Bennet from the charge of murder. In light of this, the collector's reaction seemed completely inexplicable to the inspector, at least at first.

Before he made his way to Judge Owen's house, he asked Jacob Young to find the doctor for the case. Gordon Craig offered to do the search and bring Young to the crime scene. Dorian Bayley had noticed him very upset, as if he was on the verge of recovery. He agreed that he was the one to go and invited him to look for Father Beathan as well for a farewell.

Darkness had already fallen in *Greystone* and, along with it, disturbing ghosts had come down to tear people from their homes. In such a small community, news of the second murder had travelled faster than lightning; a large group of people had gathered in the space in front of the gate of Judge Owen's villa with torches in their hands, as if it were a mystical recurrence. A tall, burly man, whom Bayley had already glimpsed in the days leading up to the Golden Pub, placed his torch on the ground and raised his arms wide open to the sky.

'We will be the next victims,' he shouted, trying in a solemn and grave tone to give importance to his words, 'look around, everyone invokes his own extinct demon. We must put an end to this infamous practice. We must leave the demons in the underworld and live our earthly life without bartering their returns for some more terrifying murder.'

Many of those present nodded, while from the path that came out of the wood you could see someone in half-light who, with a slow pace, was approaching the villa. When he came close to the others, some of those present stretched their torches towards that figure; Madame Eleonor's face appeared from the shadow.

'You,' cried the burly man, increasingly fomented, pointing to the new coming, 'witch of the devil. It was you who awakened the demons who hunt us. And now you will pay for all the bloodshed.'

The man made his way through the small crowd and with an angry impulse tried to reach Madame Eleanor with nefarious intentions. Jacob Young sprang along with two other men who were in the vicinity, among them Dorian Bayley recognized Deven Bell, the friend Martin Ford had introduced him to before the start of the treasure hunt, and they managed to get in a moment before the man struck the seer, holding him back with difficulty.

Sarah Benson, who came out of nowhere, immediately went to see the seer's condition while most of the people present wandered around without a precise direction, creating macabre plays of light with their torches, each invoking his own God or his own demon.

Dorian Bayley called his agent back. On the gate of the house, making sure no one entered the villa, was Mayor Chapman.

'You're welcome,' he said to Dorian Bayley as he opened the gate to let them through, 'I'm available for anything.'

Dr Burlow arrived in a moment, also warned by a fellow countryman, while Father Beathan arrived in the company of Gordon Craig a few minutes later, wearing the sacred vestments and ready to give the last comfort to the young victim.

The judge's house had been ransacked and traces of blood had been left all over the place, a sign that the killer hadn't even bothered to rinse his bloody hands in search of the manuscript.

'What can you tell me, Dr Burlow?' Bayley asked once outside the house, always in the company of Jacob Young.

'On first examination, I don't rule out the possibility that it could be the same person who killed Vernon Doyle. The only difference is that this time it didn't affect the body.'

'Perhaps it's because he's focused on his main mission,' the inspector pointed out, 'leaving aside the sadistic satisfaction of going after that poor girl.'

The doctor nodded, then went back.

'Margaret Strain was killed from behind with a knife or a very sharp weapon and she didn't even try to defend herself, as she blindly trusted the person she had just welcomed into the house.'

'So,' Inspector made it clear, 'Margaret opened up to her killer and made way for him to sit in the lounge. We are certain that she knew him and that he had already been in this house. Suddenly the guest pulled out a knife and slit her throat by grabbing her behind. Then he searched everywhere until he found what he was looking for and finally escaped without inflicting harm on the body, perhaps because he was afraid, or knew, that Judge Owen would return shortly thereafter.'

'I would say that this reconstruction holds up,' confirmed the pathologist thoughtfully, 'as soon as I examine the corpse in the morgue I can be more precise and give you confirmation of what has just been said.'

30 October 1884 – Thursday

As he made his way to Nevil Morgan's house, Dorian Bayley felt a fierce anger growing inside him; in his long career he couldn't remember a case where a second murder occurred when he was about to catch the killer and bring him to justice. So if it was Adam Ford who had killed, he had done it before his eyes, almost in defiance. The seemingly grumpy and naive man had skilfully evaded Jacob Young's guard, demonstrating refined intelligence and ruthless action. The brazenness with which he had carried out another brutal murder confirmed both the dangerousness and the cunning of a behaviour planned down to the smallest detail. The murderer was acting according to a precise plan, protected by accomplices able to guarantee him a safe escape route once the task was completed. The sale of the four manuscripts would have allowed him to enjoy a luxurious life in a faraway country without the risk of being caught.

In those moments Dorian Bayley felt the investigation slip from his hands; he realized he had taken too many things for granted and made the unforgivable mistake of underestimating his enemies. As if that were not enough, he regretted having placed too much faith in the investigative abilities of two inexperienced officers who, until the day he arrived at *Greystone*, had never dealt with crimes of that magnitude. He also blamed himself for not paying attention to all the warnings that the investigation had left him on the street like bread crumbs.

Since the discovery of Vernon Doyle's body, in fact, he had begun to live with a latent discomfort that he felt pulsating behind the back of his neck, that sort of sixth sense that in the past had helped him to unravel skeins without apparent logic. He had the impression that an invisible entity preceded him wherever he went and built a deformed reality around him, clouding his reason with distorted images.

He pointed his feet in the snow and observed an indefinite point on the horizon; he cleared his mind by exhaling vehemently, eliminated every tinsel that had intoxicated his reason and reconstructed every single event by framing it with the sole aid of logic. The case required immediate action. The time for waiting was over. The clues in his hand pointed in the direction of Adam Ford, but now he knew there was more. A perfect game of interlocking, the rules of which had been created by minds of superior intelligence. From now on, he would never leave out the slightest detail.

On the day of the first inspection at Morgan's house his sixth sense had communicated something to him, a reality hidden behind the appearance that normal senses showed him.

When he was about to enter that garden again the first impression was of a beautiful cottage surrounded by greenery. He first checked the windows and the lock of the only door overlooking the garden again. He managed to enter with the same system used the first time, not before making sure that there were no even imperceptible scratches in the patch. Apart from the dust accumulated on the furniture and the table, the ground floor was in order and nothing was missing. One of the two anomalies he remembered, however, was upstairs, on the desk. The side drawers were accessible, while the central drawer had a lock and was left closed. A detail that had not gone unnoticed by the inspector and showed that someone had sneaked into Nevil Morgan's house after his disappearance; he knew what to look for and where, but had made the mistake of closing the drawer after stealing its contents. Other than that, the theft had turned out to be a real professional. What had been stolen must have been of great value, although Dorian Bayley was not sure whether it was the manuscript. Even on the patch of the chest of drawers there were no streaks or scratches, so the thief must have used a copy of the key or the previously stolen original.

He got up and went down the stairs, positioning himself in a place from where he could get an overview of the ground floor. The space developed in length, with a regular plan that delimited a single room. Just to the right, a round table with three chairs rested on a beige carpet and created a cosy corner near a fireplace finished in stone. On the walls, two compartmentalized furniture contained a large number of books, while paintings depicting unspoilt nature hung on the open spaces. On a small desk in the corner, a series of carefully arranged miniature objects, perhaps the result of a passion for collecting, were displayed. On the back wall, finally, stood a bookcase that was set as if it had been made to measure. The inspector walked back and forth several times, trying to notice something that might arouse his curiosity. Again, his sixth sense woke up and began to pulsate behind the back of his neck.

'Of course!' He cried out by planting himself in the middle of the room.

He went out and stopped outside, near the corner that marked the beginning of the long side of the room. He walked the entire length of the room counting the steps, then went back and repeated the operation. He returned to the house, leaned against the wall and counted the

steps that separated it from the opposite one. There was no doubt about it: the size of the room was at least two steps smaller than the outer wall that delimited it.
'A room kept secret,' concluded between himself.
He approached the embedded cabinet and examined it carefully, passing every visible crevice with his fingers. He put pressure in some places by approaching the ear, being careful not to make a noise. When he reached the left corner, he moved the desk, taking care not to drop the objects, put the palms of his hands in the same point in the middle and the pressure he exerted triggered a click. A part of the bookcase, big just little less than the size of an average-sized man, moved a few inches. He took the books off the shelf and put his hand in; with his fingertips he hooked an invisible recess inlaid in the wood of the furniture, which he used to pull the door he had just discovered.
Inside was the secret world of Nevil Morgan. His soul projected into an elusive, mysterious dimension, regulated by the supernatural and magic. Dorian Bayley knew that Nevil Morgan was an eccentric man, but he discovered only now that his entire life was governed by mysticism. The closet resembled a small occult museum; besides various exotic objects, fetishes, candles and esoteric manuscripts, two long hooded cloaks, one black and one red, were placed on a coat rack. On the back of the dark one was sewn a strange yellow cross, with the four asymmetrical sides made up of intertwined lines tightly woven in the centre by transversal lace. The rays of the cross did not join at the centre, but left a square space also composed of intertwined lines of the same colour as the flowering wheat. On the back of the red cloak, on the other hand, was a woman with a serene gaze, wearing a long, tight-fitting dress that highlighted her graceful forms

and a cape that descended gently over her shoulders. The figure stretched her arms forward and held a basket. On the more hidden side, there were wooden snow crampons and a small door of about twenty inches set on the wall at eye level. Inside Dorian Bayley found a wooden book holder with two supports at the base. The contents had disappeared; it was safe to assume that it was the third manuscript. To complete the collection, the murderer had no choice but to steal only one more.

***

'Martin, I need to talk to you.'
Left Inspector Morgan's house, Dorian Bayley headed straight for the Fords' house. He had been seated in a chair by the burning fireplace. The boy, distressed and frightened by the affair, was holding a half-full glass of Brandy in his hand. At that moment, his mother was in town on an errand.
'Inspector, you must believe me, I don't know where my father is.'
'Right now I want to know why you broke into Nevil Morgan's house after he disappeared; what were you looking for that was so important?'
The boy's face turned white as milk.
'What are you...what are you saying? I've never been in that house, I've never stolen anything in my life.'
'Martin,' calmly resumed the inspector, 'I know you had nothing to do with this story, but I know you were involved in it game force. Your father is facing some very serious charges, so you better stop lying to me.'
Martin Ford started feeling cornered. He knew the inspector wasn't bluffing this time.

'The day you followed me, remember? I checked the footprints left on the snow. They match your foot size perfectly. Yesterday, when you left the house while I was talking to your father at the door, you left some on the ground, and then I had no doubt. Moreover, only two people in the village are familiar with locks and keys and George Davies has a completely different physical shape. But it was he who told me he had you as an apprentice when you were a teenager. He is the only locksmith in town and in his workshop there are only two models of locks, one for large furniture and one for writing desks and desks. It must have been easy to make a duplicate key and leave no trace. It would have been a perfect theft if you hadn't made the mistake of locking the drawer once you took the contents. Who would keep an empty one under lock and key? I also know that you only took a part of the loot that day; when you came back to finish the job, however, you noticed I was there and fled in a hurry. Now I need you to tell me everything you know.'

The boy drank the Brandy all in one sip and plunged with his back into the upholstered back of the armchair, exhaling as if he had held his breath for a minute.

'I don't know where my father's hiding, but you're right, he's the one who convinced me to make a copy of the key and retrieve a diary and a manuscript from Inspector Morgan's house. I knew where to look, but someone beat me to it. I managed to get the diary but the book was already gone. Before you ask, I don't know what's in the diary. I gave it to my father without opening it. But perhaps you should follow me. I'll show you something that will help you with your investigation.'

They put on their coats and went out into the garden; they passed the cemetery and headed towards a path that was lost in the woods, stopping first in a shed that served as a storehouse for work tools.

'Put these on,' Martin addressed the inspector with a pair of snow crampons while he did the same. 'The path is quite winding.'

Dorian Bayley put them on and took a few steps; the crampons adhered well to the soles of the shoes and left regular footprints deeper than they would have formed without them. Martin Ford made his way holding a stick in his hand, while the inspector positioned himself to his left.

'Where are we headed?'

'South to the Wilsons and Father Beathan's house; from there we have to go up through the woods to the big pastures, continue and cross the fence that marks out Judge Owen's property.'

Even in this area the vegetation was so dense that the sun's rays could not penetrate. The path descended almost immediately into a silent half-light and the cold became pungent.

'My father is an honest man, Inspector, and a hard worker. He doesn't like company and has a bad temper. That, however, does not make him a murderer,' the boy said.

'Tell me everything you know,' he merely reiterated Dorian Bayley.

'On the day of the robbery at my house, I received a telegram from my father, begging me to return to *Greystone* as a matter of urgency. I got worried and left that same evening. When I saw him at the station it was no longer him; more than a manuscript seemed to have taken a son away from him. In a very confused way, he told me of a danger we were in and the need to act without hesitation to prevent it. From an early age I noticed in him a strange inclination for esotericism; he often frequented the house of Madame Eleonor, a half-crazy old lady who lives in the woods and many consider to be a seer. He also has contacts with Judge Owen and Mayor Chapman, which is strange given their social class difference. I often saw Inspector Morgan around the house, too, and at one point, I began to consider him family.'

'Why did your father have ongoing relations with these people?'

Martin Ford spread his arms.

'Until shortly before I left *Greystone,* it was never clear to me. Then my father told me a secret with the promise that I would never share it with anyone else. But the dangerous situation we're in now forces me to break that promise.'

'If you want to help me catch the culprit, there's no other way,' encouraged Dorian Bayley.

'*Greystone* is not the quiet, prosperous town that appears in the eyes of a stranger. Behind the smiling faces lie unspeakable secrets. The inhabitants are victims of strange forms of superstition and act only on the faith they embrace. You have already had an idea of this yourself and if you read the local chronicles you will discover that often, in the woods, clear traces of black masses, animal sacrifices, crosses, satanic symbols and suchlike have been found. My father Adam Ford, Mayor Montgomery Chapman, Judge Frank Owen and Inspector Nevil Morgan are part of a sect that practices a form of magic linked to the ancient Celtic religion. They consider themselves to be the repositories of a knowledge with which they would be able to counteract the evil forces from the underworld. Thanks to my parents I was able to leave *Greystone* when I was very young; I studied medicine in London and later moved to Liverpool, where I work as a medical assistant. I never believed in magic, so what I tell you has only historical value.'

'Do you think your father's disappearance is connected to what you're telling me?'

'I'm sure of it. In addition to the stories I've been told, I've been personally informed. The Celts celebrated the end of the harvest and the arrival of winter with the rite of Samhain. It was considered an ambivalent period, full of suggestions and full of magic. Popular belief believes that only once a year, on the night between 31 October and 1 November, the gap separating the world of the dead from that of the living opens up and allows the former to visit their loved ones. According to even more ancient beliefs, however, in addition to the quiet souls of the dead, there are dark entities that try to cross the door in order to plunge the world into eternal darkness and a state of primordial chaos. They are demons who impersonate evil in its purest form. The followers of the sect are vigilant that evil does not pass through the door and the natural order of the universe is maintained.'

'Are you telling me that your father escaped capture and hid just to perform a magical ritual?'

'Knowing him I think so, although the disappearance of the manuscripts complicates matters; the formula for celebrating it is hidden in those four books and as far as I know there are no other copies in the world.'

The path opened and they found themselves in the middle of expanses of fields used by shepherds to graze their flocks. They continued to walk for a few minutes until they resumed the path that climbed in an easterly direction from the centre of the village; finally, they arrived in front of a fence.

'This is where Judge Owen's estate begins. We need to get over the fence by committing a minor trespass on private property, but I think the end justifies this little gamble. We're going to go about three miles over there to the clearing that opens up into the woods.'

Apart from the fence, which for the most part was covered by low moss vegetation, the forest continued uninterrupted. The last part of the walk was done in silence, trying to shelter from the cold and avoiding the snow falling from the loaded branches.

The space opened for a few hundred yards and the shape resembled an irregular ellipse. To the left, where trunk trees created a wall about thirty yards high, thick creepers descended, which resembled a huge theatre curtain pulled down.

The inspector continued to follow Martin, who had approached the wall and seemed to be looking for something.

'This way,' he pointed to him by taking a few steps backwards.

He took two torches hidden in the bush and passed them to the inspector. Then he pointed out to him a point, stretched out both arms and with his hands joined in prayer opened a narrow passage between the knotty plants. He waited for the inspector to be behind him and dropped them behind them. They found themselves inside a cave. The environment was dark and there was only a strong smell of moisture and soot.

Martin took one of the torches, lit it and did the same with the one the inspector was holding. They found themselves along a very narrow corridor dug into the rock, which they walked in single file. Dorian Bayley's disbelief was matched only by his curiosity. They crossed the tunnel until a huge chamber opened up in front of them.

'This was the original entrance to the cave; over the centuries it has been closed and hidden with spontaneous vegetation. It is considered a sacred place, the point of contact between the worlds and it is here that the Druids, the ancient Celtic priests, came to pray to their divinities.'

'Incredible,' exclaimed Dorian Bayley, who began to inspect it as carefully as a visitor in a museum room. On the walls were scattered engraved drawings of anthropomorphic beings and geometric symbols. Together they gave the idea of a continuous scene, even if the meanings were obscure. At the end of the room there was a corridor that was lost in the bowels of the earth.

'Follow me a short distance; this place is a labyrinth and inside are a series of secondary tunnels that even I don't know where they lead.'

The atmosphere you breathed was something shocking. That place seemed like the gateway to another dimension. Aside from the dripping sound coming from a few openings in the rock and short whistles generated by the wind wedged between the walls, the silence was deadly. Dorian Bayley could hear the sound of fire from the burning torch. His senses were suddenly heightened.

'Now to the right,' pointed to Martin and proceeded with confidence.

'How come you know this cave so well?'

'My father wanted me to get to know it and learn what it meant to him and the cult it's a part of. Maybe that's the real reason why he decided to adopt me. When I was a child, I used to come here with him and Inspector Morgan. Once I also saw Madame Eleanor with Mayor Chapman and the judge; they wore long votive capes and looked as if they were celebrating prayers.

Once through the tunnel, the space opened up again. A catacomb had been carved out of a smaller, longer hall. On the side walls, dug into the rock, there were beds full of pots piled up between them.

'Being part of an esoteric sect led to excommunication,' explained Martin, 'and when a member died he was cremated and placed in a funeral urn. Their remains are kept in this room.'

The room ended with the street dividing into two corridors. At the intersection, Martin turned left but Dorian Bayley beckoned him to stop.

'Wait, I hear something.'

'What?' Martin asked, turning around.

'Lead the way this way.'

As they entered, a stronger and stronger smell invaded their nostrils. At a certain moment it became so pungent that they had to cover their noses and mouths with a handkerchief. At the bottom, the tunnel was divided into three more corridors. Dorian Bayley continued to follow the smell and came to the end of a narrow, dead-end tunnel. He raised his torch to make light; lying on the wall, as if someone had left him sitting and then his body had slowly slipped, Nevil Morgan's corpse was in an advanced state of putrefaction, although his swollen face had not yet lost its original features.

'My goodness!!!' Martin Ford exclaimed horrified, closing his eyes and looking the other way.

'Another mystery solved,' said Dorian Bayley.

'He was killed the day he disappeared and his body hidden in this cave. The murderer was planning to come back and bury him who knows where, but he was killed in turn. Martin,' turned to the boy who had been petrified with fear, 'show me where the entrance is, then we will recover the body.'

'My God,' Adam Ford's son kept repeating in a trembling voice as he made his way away from what had become Inspector Morgan's grave.

As they walked they came to an irregular room; at the bottom, some steps had been carved out of the rock and ended in front of a sealed door.

'This secret door leads to the church library,' said Martin Ford.

'That's where the killer escaped from,' exclaimed astonished Dorian Bayley.

They climbed the stairs in single file; when they were at the top Martin pulled a lever hidden in a recess on the right. A blade of light filtered down the three sides of the door; with a slight pressure it opened outwards.

'This church was built about two centuries ago, using the perimeter of the old Celtic sanctuary, a stone building whose remains are still visible outside. It was the practice of the church to try to eliminate every symbol considered pagan, often engulfing it within the new Christian creed. The secret story tells that the members of the sect, persecuted and forced to take refuge in the woods, secretly built in the rock the room that connects the cave to what is now the library, and this in order not to disperse the magic they considered pervading this space, origin and fulcrum of their religion, whose energy had to be channelled during the battles against the demons.'

While listening to Martin's words, Dorian Bayley studied its conformation; the mechanism was similar to the one discovered in Inspector Morgan's house. The secret door was hidden in a bookcase cabinet divided into internal shelves. This, however, could only be opened from the cave and not vice versa.

'That's why I couldn't find it when I inspected the library,' the inspector thought, 'and that explains the origin of the soil found near the body and near the altar. Nevil Morgan must have discovered almost immediately that Vernon Doyle was responsible for the theft. He was interested in recovering the manuscript first. On the day of his disappearance, he used the secret passage and entered the library leaving the door open, as he had decided to use the passage also to escape. He met Vernon Doyle, whether by chance or not, and attacked and killed him. In panic Vernon Doyle took the corpse, wrapped it in a cotton cloth so as not to leave traces of blood and dragged it down the stairs and hid it in a safe place. He returned to the library and closed the door without realising he could never open it again. Ignoring where the entrance to the cave was, he could no longer retrieve the corpse. Before he could get organized, however, he was killed himself a few days later. His murderer collected the dirt under the soles of his shoes because he also came from the cave and left it on the floor during the fight. The one I found the day the body was discovered matches exactly what is accumulated under the crampons. Unlike Vernon Doyle, however, the second murderer had the foresight to leave the door open and was able to escape undisturbed. Martin, go call Gordon and Jacob right away and have them come here in a carriage. We need to transport the inspector's body to the cemetery morgue. I'll be honest with you, these new leads only confirm my suspicions about your father. If he tries to contact you, convince him to turn himself in so as not to aggravate the situation. I won't let any more people get killed.'

'I understand, Inspector, but I remain convinced of my father's innocence. I'm running to warn your officers,' he said before he started running with his hat in his hand.

***

When Dorian Bayley arrived at the cemetery morgue a few hours later, he found Dr Burlow who had just finished analysing the two bodies. He still had his shirt sleeves rolled up and a long brown leather apron tied around his waist. The room was huge and bare; some large blocks of ice placed in the corners kept the ideal temperature to preserve the bodies from rapid decay. A large central chandelier illuminated the steel beds on which the victims' bodies were lying, while the rest of the room remained shrouded in semi-darkness.

After washing his hands, the pathologist took off his apron, adjusted his sleeves and put on his jacket.

'Found something, Dr Burlow?' The inspector asked as he glanced at the victims.

The doctor's face was worn out.

'I've analysed the bodies superficially, of course, but I can confirm that Margaret Strain bled to death from a deep throat cut, while Inspector Nevil Morgan was killed with a blunt force trauma that nearly smashed his skull in the back. Death must have come for both of them almost instantaneously.'

'Two very different ways of killing,' said the inspector as he examined the wounds.

Dr Burlow pointed at the woman's neck.

'The meat in this area has a laceration compatible with a knife with a very thick blade. Although I have to carry out some analysis and comparisons, the wound has the same angle as the one found on Vernon Doyle's body. This victim was also cut from right to left, but with less force. It's clear that the killer's intent was to kill. In the case of Inspector Morgan, on the other hand, the dynamic suggests an instinctive and unforeseen action; perhaps a sudden raptus triggered a blind and ferocious rage. The poor woman's body was still warm and death can be less than an hour before her discovery, while Inspector Morgan must have been killed a few days ago. It is difficult to determine exactly when; the degree of humidity and bacteria present in a cave can alter the timing of a normal post-mortem decomposition process. I'll be more precise about that, too, after studying the two bodies.'

'From right to left,' reflected Dorian Bayley.

'There's no doubt about it,' the pathologist echoed.

'He slit both their throats but only attacked Vernon Doyle's body. Why do you think that is?'

'Hard to say. It's possible that in Vernon Doyle's case the killer felt the need to discharge a repressed anger that had suddenly been unleashed and continued to rage until he quenched his bloodlust. As for the woman, however, there is the possibility that the killer had not planned to kill her, but was eliminated because she accidentally found herself in his way. I won't deny that I'd be very interested in studying such a twisted mind.'

'A man who is out of control and very dangerous, who wants to achieve a goal and eliminate any obstacle he faces. You were right when you talked about a mission to accomplish. A mission that unfortunately has not yet been completed. He must be stopped before he commits another massacre.'

'I'm afraid, Inspector, that the culprit will do anything not to get caught. Pay the utmost attention.'

'Do not doubt Dr Burlow. Good evening and thank you for the information,' Dorian Bayley greeted as he touched his hat cutter.

'Good evening to you, Inspector,' replied the pathologist as he wore the black top hat with his left hand and headed for the exit, where a carriage was ready to take him back to the village.

31 October 1884 – Friday

'Jacob, come to my office in five minutes,' the inspector told his officer immediately after entering the station.

Inside the stove was on and the room was warm. He took off his coat and hat, poured water into the teapot and from his jacket pocket he pulled out an elegant cigar holder. As he placed it on his desk he noticed two sealed envelopes; the larger one came from London, the smaller one from *Little Castle*. He did not have time to put the water on to warm up, and Jacob knocked.

'Come on in.'

'Inspector, I arrived very early this morning and took the liberty of lighting the stove. I also left two packages on your desk, a letter from Scotland Yard and an urgent telegram.'

'Listen to me Jacob: Adam Ford has escaped, we don't know where he is, but we know what he is looking for; I have reason to believe that the fourth book is in Mayor Chapman's possession, even though he has guaranteed me that he knows nothing about it. What kind of game these three people are playing, I still don't understand it, but I need you and Gordon to go to him and protect him in case someone shows up with bad intentions. Unfortunately, I don't have the power to take him to the station or search his house. But I can certainly make sure nothing happens to him. I want you to be armed. Call Gordon and get ready.'

'Yes, sir.'

Leaving, the officer walked out the door and closed it. Dorian Bayley took the opportunity to dedicate himself to his morning ritual. He finished cutting the cigar, took a cup, poured the tea leaves and flooded them with boiling water. As he lit the cigar, he enjoyed the aroma of tobacco as it spread. He opened the envelope from London; inside a document contained the results of a chemical analysis that the inspector had requested on the grassy residue found on a shelf in the library on the day of the first murder. He looked through all the parts that did not interest him and went straight to the second page, where there was a list of the components; he read it and found the confirmation he was looking for: Dover dust and laudanum. He set aside the file and opened the envelope from *Little Castle* with a knife; it was an urgent telegram sent by Edmund Vinson, the famous art expert and historian. He picked up the paper with his left hand, while with his right hand he continued sipping tea; he read the text, which he recited:

– *The original is written in archaic Greek (stop)* –

'Greek, not Latin,' he whispered with an air of surprise.

He was petrified; the cup slipped from his hands and ended up on the floor, flooding the floor with tea and fragments of earthenware.

He recovered and hastened to recall the two agents.

'Listen carefully: run to the mayor's house and stay there until I get back.'

'Where are you going in the meantime?' Gordon Craig asked as he finished adjusting his uniform and checked the condition of the revolver.

'I'm going to put an end to the murders.'

***

Dorian Bayley hadn't come very far. After he left his room, he came down the steps that led him to the basement.

'Finally,' said Darrel Bennet when he saw him, 'I just wanted to talk to you.'

A quarter of an hour later, after leaving the building, he took Main Street and stopped in front of the old trough, where he checked that the gun was loaded. The icy morning air entered his lungs like many sharp blades. Now that the circle was about to close, everything seemed linear, as if the clues had gone into place by inertia. The weight that gripped him began to lighten; within two days he would return to London, taking with him all the sensations that had accompanied him to *Greystone,* as well as a load of beer brewed by Tom Porter.

He continued at a slow pace to avoid falling on the icy road, looking for safe handholds and helping himself, where he could, passing under arcades or on the sides, where the snow was piled up and kept soft. The people he crossed kept his head bent over; every now and then someone would hint at a distracted greeting. In St. Patrick Square he turned for King's road, passed the inn and pulled straight ahead until he got lost in the woods. He saw the boundary wall of the cemetery peeping through the trees bent by the snow, which descended copiously all night long. He promised himself that, as soon as he returned to London, he would buy two pairs of crampons; the shoes he was wearing were now to be sent to the pulping yard.

He continued to savour the silence of unspoilt nature. He was certain that the purity of the fresh snow would cleanse the country of all the bloodshed. An indelible sign would remain forever but a scar would take the place of a bleeding wound, and this would be enough to make people's souls quiet.

He saw two houses in the distance. He approached and, in the garden on the left, observed a little girl playing with a puppy dog. The door was open and from time to time the mother would stop on the edge to check that everything was all right. When she saw the inspector approaching, she stared at him as if awaiting instructions. Dorian Bayley beckoned to let the child in and continued on. There was so much smoke coming out of the chimneys of the houses that they looked like the chimneys of locomotives being thrown at great speed.

He entered the garden through the back. The window curtains were drawn, so he bent down on his knees and walked in small steps so as not to be seen. He put the revolver in an easy-to-reach spot on the belt. Around the corner was the only entrance door. He stood up and decided that the best thing was not to sneak in, but to knock like a courtesy visit. He was certain he hadn't created suspicion of any kind. In the minds of every villager the fugitive to be sought was Adam Ford, the manuscript theft and murderer. His accomplice was in prison. There was no need to worry about the others, since they were under close surveillance.

He knocked on the door after resuming his normal relaxed appearance.

He heard footsteps approaching; he was sure to find him.

'Good morning, Inspector, I'm pleased to see you. Come in and have a cup of hot tea.'

'Good morning Father Beathan,' replied Dorian Bayley as he took off his hat and entered the house.

***

The priest sat the inspector down, closed the door and went into the kitchen. He came out with two steaming cups of tea, which he placed on the table. Dorian Bayley grabbed one without saying thank you; he stared at the man in front of him, stripped of his holy clothes, with his features changed now that the mask he was wearing had melted like wax on the fire. His gaze had lost that aura of goodness which he was able to convey with such natural skill, turning into a sinister, evil expression; his smile bent into a frosty grimace, when only five minutes earlier it had widened like a white sheet stretched out to dry. Without the dress Joseph Beathan displayed a well-structured and muscular body.

'Do you have any news, Inspector? I was just finishing getting ready to go to church.'

'Father Beathan, where were you the night Vernon Doyle was killed?'

The priest's face became purple; all he could do was gibberish:

'For... Why... Why this question, Inspector?'

Dorian Bayley wouldn't stop staring at him, ready to draw his weapon if he noticed the slightest suspicious movement.

'Please answer me, Father.'

'Perhaps you doubt my honesty?' The prelate tried to defend by putting his hands together and bringing them near his mouth.

'I need an answer,' urged the inspector.

As if he was beginning to run out of air, the priest trained his shirt collar and began to breathe with difficulty; he took two steps back until he collapsed into the armchair. He closed his eyes and began to pray, whispering something.

The inspector unbuttoned his coat and put his hand near the revolver.

'It wasn't easy, you turned out to be as cunning as a weasel. If you had acted differently, maybe I could have saved that poor girl's life. But it was her death that made me solve the case. You made only two mistakes, almost negligible; in the fight with Vernon Doyle you did not realize that you had lost a letter from your medallion, the symbol of the omega, which ended up on the ground near the corpse. I was wrong to trust my knowledge, because I was convinced that the sentence in the Anglican rose, which reads "the truth will make you free" was written in Latin. When I began to suspect you, however, so as not to be too conspicuous, I had a telegram sent to Professor Vinson. Last night I received his reply, in which he informed me that the first Anglicans did not use Latin but Greek. When I came to visit you, then, I saw that you kept more medallions in the house but had stopped wearing them around your neck since the day of the first murder, perhaps for fear that I might notice the detail.

Father Beathan seemed not to listen; he was curled up on himself and continued to recite his litany with his eyes closed, swinging with his body and trying to hold back a tremor that spread from his hands and up his arms.

As if nothing had happened, Dorian Bayley resumed the story, almost as if to put his head in order.

'Alone, however, this clue would not have been enough; yesterday's visit, however, proved very useful. Knowing that you keep dangerous clues at home, you had the foresight in these days to never be found there. In the bedroom there was a crampon, the left one; the wood at the base is darker in colour than the sole, a sign that it has been used recently, while near the entrance hangs the right one, which has all the wood of the same lighter colour. It was you who followed me into the woods the first time I went to visit Madame Eleonor and it was you who attacked me near the inn. The next morning I got up early to go and study the footprints you had left as you fled; they were equally deep, while a man who limps leaves a less pronounced one. You were brilliant in wearing only a crampon, the left one, so that no one could attribute those footprints to an individual with a crippled leg to a visual analysis.

Then there was the mystery of which hand the killer used to kill. Dr Burlow determined that the blows were all delivered in the same direction from left to right. Analysing the elements found in the library and the church, I had imagined that the killer had approached the victim head-on, taking advantage of the darkness, and struck the blow with his right hand; Vernon Doyle did not even have time to mention a defence. Once on the ground, you positioned yourself over the corpse and struck two more stab wounds to the abdomen. I immediately wondered why that unnecessary fury and why, above all, the subsequent blows were delivered with less force and precision. The answer was clear: they were used to muddy the waters and to make one think that the killer was left-handed. To do so, it was sufficient to change hands. Vernon Doyle was already a corpse, so you were able to take the time to set the scene. But it wasn't until I saw how Margaret Strain died that I knew I was wrong. The maid opened the door, greeted you and turned to make her way to the salon. You rushed at her, grabbed her with your right hand at the waist and slit her throat using the other one. During the funeral ceremony I saw you turn the pages of the Gospel with your left hand; no one would use the other hand to make a mechanical gesture. Vernon Doyle stole the manuscript from Adam Ford's house at your request; believing he could do who knows what, he decided to perform the ritual using part of the magic formula contained in it. To stimulate the senses and fall into an altered phase of consciousness, he prepared a drink in which he dissolved hallucinogenic substances. Panicked and, perhaps, from hallucinations, he fled to the church and started to invoke the Lord's forgiveness in front of the altar. At that moment, you came out of the dark corner where you had hidden yourself and killed him by cutting his throat from behind. You did so because you had realized you could no longer trust him and knew that you would soon be discovered and forced to confess. I don't know how, but you are aware of the existence of the cave inside Judge Owen's property and you know that one of the corridors leads to behind the library. It was easy to use it to get to the church and escape without the risk of being discovered. The mistake that nailed you, however,' he concluded as he drew his gun, 'was made yesterday when you came to the police station; I'm sure you did it not to talk to me but to try to figure out what suspicions I had and what moves I was making, but above all it was an excuse to sneak into the basement and talk to Darrel Bennet, reassuring him that only one book was missing from the entire collection that he would have paid you in gold. Realizing your strategy, I led you astray by telling you about Adam Ford, whom I already knew to be innocent. In order not to take risks, I didn't even inform my agents, who could have missed something given the persuasive power you seem to have with the villagers and the ease with which they open up to you. You expressed the wish that the perpetrator of these horrendous crimes would soon be brought to justice. At that moment I had the final intuition; how did you know that there had been a second murder if Margaret Strain's body had not yet been discovered by Judge Owen? Only the killer could have known about it, no one else. Using the plural, you accused yourself of being the author of all the horror *Greystone* has experienced over the last two weeks. Father Beathan, you're a psychopath, and the motive for the money you would have earned from selling the entire collection seems pretty convincing to me, but you're not the only one. While searching the house I noticed that it contains several anthropological texts and some that deal with ancient religions; I have the impression that over time you have acquired the conviction that one could manipulate nature and gain advantage from it by selling his soul to a demon, betraying his belief and sinking into a paranoid search for a way to immortality. A mission that led you to lose contact with reality and turn into an unscrupulous killer, in which innocent people turned into simple obstacles to overcome. It will be the judge to establish the right punishment; for my part, I condemn without extenuating circumstances any individual who overrules his fellow man, who abuses his position and who suppresses an innocent life. Now please follow me to the police station.'

Father Beathan lifted his gaze; his red eyes were wet with copious tears streaming down his cheeks and marked by deep dark circles under the eyes. The impression was that of a man no longer present.

'I have lived following the path drawn by God, in righteousness, asking every evening for forgiveness for my sins, setting the power of prayer against the sensual fluids of the devil, always ready to corrupt souls and to promise in return every kind of earthly pleasure. But man is weak and often faces an unequal battle, which he is not always able to win. Inspector, my faith is strong and in every moment I have lived I have felt God's closeness. I have acted trying to bring goodness and a word of comfort to anyone in need, without asking anything in return, except to try to be happy and in communion with the Lord. But for a long time, darkness has fallen in my heart;

I have lost every path and my soul wanders in the arid desert of solitude. I had to take the lives of two innocent people because only in this way I had a hope of finding the light; but now that I have been stopped eternal darkness has fallen within me. Yes, Inspector, I'll go with you; just give me time to collect some things I'd like to take with me.'

'I'll give you five minutes, but don't try to escape or I'll be forced to use it,' Dorian Bayley intimated to him, raising his arm and showing the revolver.

Father Beathan got up and walked towards the bedroom, while the inspector followed his movements carefully. Although the priest seemed docile and lacking in energy, he was still a sick and therefore unpredictable man. The words he had just spoken confirmed his descent into madness and his religious fervour was in danger of turning into a dangerous detonator always ready to set off ferocious violence.

Dorian Bayley, who had remained on the threshold of the bedroom, heard a noise behind him and turned around; he saw nothing and thought it was the cat Father Beathan kept in the house. At that moment, the bedroom door closed and you could hear the key turn twice. Dorian Bayley ran out into the garden and reached the back window. The curtain was closed; he came back into the house and tried to understand what was happening. The priest had always killed with a knife, so it was not possible that he had a gun in the house. But the man had demonstrated great intelligence, and now that he had been discovered he could be more dangerous than a wounded lion in a trap. He heard the screech of a chair being dragged across the floor, then some noises of tools that he couldn't make out. He remained motionless for a few interminable seconds, then decided that the best thing was to break into the room. Fortunately for him, the door was made of light wood, and a strong push would have been enough to blow the lock off. He put the revolver to his belt and prepared himself; as he prepared to enter he heard a dull noise and immediately something was vibrating. He took a slight recourse and threw himself into the door; his violent shoulder blew the hinges off and Dorian Bayley managed to get in and threw the door to the ground. He looked into the middle of the room and was surprised, almost astonished. Father Beathan's helpless body was now hanging from the ceiling, hanging from a thick wicker rope with his neck broken and tongue sticking out. His lifeless eyes were injected with blood. Deciding to end his life, he had taken with him all the unspeakable truths of his crimes. In his deviant mind, perhaps, thought the inspector, that gesture had to take an extreme form of atonement. A circle of violence that had seen innocent bloodshed and ended with yet another life cut short. Thinking back on Vernon Doyle and Margaret Strain, however, Dorian Bayley failed to feel pity for Joseph Beathan.

'I entrust you to your God,' he said as he cut the rope and laid the body on the bed, 'if he really exists, he will decide the fate of your soul.'

He went out locking the door with the key and headed towards the neighbour's house; he knocked slowly so as not to frighten the woman and child.

'This is Inspector Dorian Bayley, may I disturb you? I don't know your name.'

'Alice Wilson.'

'Is your husband home?'

'He's working in the garden. He's at the back of the house.'

'Could you ask him the kindness to go into town and have my agents come? They're at Mayor Chapman's house. Tell them to bring a transport wagon.'

'I'll go right away, Inspector; would you like to come in the house? In this awful cold, you'd better get up by the fireplace.'

'Thank you, madam, but I prefer to wait outside.'

Dorian Bayley opened the cigar case and took one already cut out. He turned it on and made the first pull by half-closing his eyes and looking up to the sky. Waiting for his men to arrive to take the body away, he let himself be captured by the memories and the hint of a warm tear came out of his wet eyes.

To stop thinking he had to walk; darkness had fallen without him noticing. Outside the windowsills were lit candles that lit bowls containing bread and cheese and jugs full of water; Bayley did not understand the reason, but that evocative image remained with him all evening, distracting him from his saddest memories.

31 October 1750

'The lines of time are about to join and return to their point of origin; soon the dimensional gates will align and create the gap between the worlds. But this is the night of the Third Mother, when the powers of evil will try to leave their damned kingdom and cross the path into our world. Let us celebrate in the sacred temple of the Gods the night of Black Samhain, let us draw from the earth the primordial energies to fight the emissaries of evil.'

A slight vibration of the ground anticipated a dull noise coming from the bowels of the earth.

Madame Althea had positioned herself in the middle and stared at a point on the rock face. The first master on the left began to whisper words incomprehensible to the ears of the others. When he finished, he raised his arms and screamed.

'I summon the soul of the underworld.'

That's when midnight struck.

The silence was interrupted by a rumble that emerged from the depths and exploded like an underground spring that after a long dark path finds its outlet outside. The floor rose like a wave, the space began to contract and expand as if it had come to life and was breathing.

The second master repeated the gestures and movements of the first, remaining motionless within the circle. After whispering his part of the formula, he clenched his fists and raised them with anger as if to hit something.

'Appear and show yourself.'

The blue flames suspended in the air became red, turning upside down and leaving a burning liquid dripping. The portion of the wall that Madame Althea could not stop staring at changed in consistency; a strong shock rained sharp rocks from the ceiling, one of which struck the man inside the fourth circle. A scream of pain was heard, which spread until it was confused with the noise of the earth, which panting ferociously like a wounded animal. The grand master managed not to break the chain; he picked up the book and the parchment, got up holding his shoulder with the other hand and resumed the initial position. Madame Althea waved her stick and the circumference of the four circles lit up as if burning with its own life.

The rock of the wall changed consistency, almost melting under a lava flow pushing from the inside. The tremors became more intense and the cave seemed about to implode on itself. Rumours and cries of terror accompanied the appearance of a blinding light, which forced the Grand Masters to protect their eyes so as not to be injured. When it stopped, an irregular opening appeared out of nowhere; a huge ravine from which came a nauseating smell of rotting bodies. The slimy blood dripping from the newly formed nave melted like acid as soon as it touched the floor.

A deformed beast's contours emerged from the bottom of the shaft. It was huge and came in heavy steps, leaving deep footprints as it passed. The upper part of the body had human features. The face was prognathous and irregular; the lack of lips showed two rows of sharp, rotten teeth, while a dense, dark liquid dripped from the sunken eye sockets. Two outgrowths came out of the frontal area of the skull, covered with sparse burnt hair. The skin of the face seemed to be attacked by the plague. The legs, similar to ram's paws, ended with two large clogs and were entirely covered with fur. The ribcage contracted, making a cavernous groan.

The demon took a few steps forward and stopped right after crossing the threshold. Its bony, long hands held two sharp blades dripping blood. Before it could venture against Madame Althea the third man repeated the movements of the other two masters; he whispered a few words and, pointing his open hands at the demon, ordered:

'I imprison you in the limbo of time, shadow of night.'

The entity screamed as if a hundred blades had pierced his body. An invisible force forced it to widen his arms, lifted it by weight and threw it against the wall, where it ended up crucified with the rock that had welded its arms and legs into the wall. The beast waved, shaking its head as if it had lost his mind, stopping only to stare at the members of the sect with an expression of visceral hatred.

Madame Althea watched the scene waiting for the last of the masters to complete the formula and reject the demon through the door; but the man lay on the ground lifeless because of the wound, which had caused him to lose a great deal of blood.

'The beast will not remain a prisoner for long,' cried the great master, 'let us absorb the energy of the mother earth to plunge it into the world of eternal darkness.'

The other three masters seemed like prisoners inside the circle, helpless as if they had fallen into a deep trance. Madame Althea cast a curse on the beast by moving the stick in its direction; a deep gash opened from the side of the demon and immediately the blood began to flow. At the same time, the superhuman effort of the entity overcame the resistance of the rock, which crumbled and left one arm free. The screams of anger tore through the damp air, carrying the desire for human blood like a pregnant odour. The demon threw the knife he was holding trying to strike Madame Althea, but the woman was quick to throw herself on her left and dodge the deadly attack. She got back on her feet and reached the unconscious man; she celebrated a formula and infused him with energy by making a cut at the level of her wrists and placing the wet wound on his lips. The grand master's face pulsed with life again. Bleeding and shaky on his legs, he managed to get on his knees, gathered the remaining strength and returned to the circle. A large boulder detached itself from the vault and hit the ground, touching it with nothing. The beast, meanwhile, had managed to free one of its legs and continued to wriggle.

'Now or it will be the end,' cried Madame Althea, gathering all her power and giving the demon a second gash on her chest.

After a moment of hesitation, the fourth man whispered the final part of the formula. The cry of the beast echoed frightfully throughout the cave. His body fell helplessly into the ground and was dragged by its paws towards the tunnel that joined the three doors. Crawling with force his huge body left a trail of black liquid on the ground, while shreds of flesh came off its face covered with infected blisters. When the darkness swallowed it up, the earth stopped shaking; the flames turned blue again, only to evaporate and disappear into thin air. Madame Althea celebrated a formula in front of the gap, which began to close with the rock slowly returning to its solid form. The nave disappeared swallowed into the wall and the blood it was impregnated with evaporated. When everything was over, the four masters were able to leave the circles and remove the cloaks burned by the fire and torn by the splinters of stone rained like bullets. Their faces were swollen and several wounds were bleeding in various parts of their bodies.

When Madame Althea announced that the beast had been defeated, she summed up her natural voice. She turned and disappeared down the shaft through which she had entered. The four masters stayed a few minutes to observe the place where good and evil had clashed in an old war born at the dawn of time and destined to perpetrate endlessly. The light would be reborn and the sun would rise again, repeating its movement relentlessly. Hope and devotion had enabled them to defeat the darkness, but they knew that soon the beast would return to bring chaos and death and thus, until the end of time, in the cyclical flow of the river of life.

1 November 1884 – Saturday

Nostalgia was often winding paths in Inspector Bayley's head. He had come to terms with a past that had not spared him the saddest enigma a father could endure; he had dragged it on for two decades, with the dignity and demeanour that could only be ascribed to great souls. Now that he was preparing to tidy up his things, in what had been his office for a few days, that nostalgia anticipated his departure. He had not spent much time in *Greystone,* but the fervour of those days, and that strange atmosphere that one breathed, had entered him with the force of a storm that left the boat at the mercy of the waves, only to calm down and deliver the sea again to the tedious monotony of its chase.

'Come in,' he answered after hearing a knock at the door.

Adam Ford appeared; from the first glance Dorian Bayley seemed to see a different person from the one he had known, or perhaps only imagined, in the days before, when all the clues led to him.

'Please come in, Mr Ford,' he said as he opened a locker and pulled out a bottle of brandy and two glasses.

'Do you keep brandy in your office?' Ford commented by wrinkling his forehead.

The inspector smiled at him.

'I may not know you very well, Mr Ford, but from what I see, the lack seems to be mutual. To what would you like to dedicate this toast?'

'To the newfound tranquillity of this village,' he replied amused.

'To the tranquillity of this magnificent village,' echoed the inspector before the glasses met in a sweet tinkle.

'To what do I owe the pleasure of this visit?'

'In the meantime, I wanted to apologize if I've been a bit gruff, but if you'll have the goodness to listen to me, I'll be able to explain to you why I did what I did. Also,' he added, 'I must give you these.'

He placed a notebook and a closed letter on the coffee table.

'This is the diary of Nevil Morgan,' the inspector noted reading the name on the cover.

'...and this is a letter that Madame Eleanor asked me to deliver to you with a prayer not to open it before you take the train to London.'

The inspector nodded; he took the letter, stood up and put it in the pocket of his coat hanger. Then he sat back down, took another sip of brandy and poured a second one to Adam Ford, who had already finished his.

'Tell me about it.'

'It all started with that damn theft,' began Adam Ford, 'as we know it was Vernon Doyle who sneaked into my house. An unsuspected man, believe me, who until that moment had never dared to do anything that was not only against the law, but that could even irritate or offend a person. Apart from being a loyal friend, Nevil Morgan was a good detective and it didn't take him long to work out who did it.'

'...went there to retrieve the stolen goods,' continued Dorian Bayley, 'or maybe he snuck in using the secret corridor, but Vernon Doyle found out and killed him with a blunt instrument.'

'It's not as simple as it looks; something more terrifying has happened.'

The inspector sensed the direction Adam Ford wanted to take in the events; he showed interest and urged him to continue.

'Vernon Doyle did a nefarious deed by reading some verses of a formula in the book. As you know, Inspector, that is one of the four manuscripts kept at *Greystone* and each of them contains the part of an ancient magic ritual, which serves to bar the way for creatures from the depths of the underworld. Every 50 years, taking advantage of favourable astral cycles, these damned souls try to cross the boundary that separates them from our world, during what the ancient Druid priests called the night of Samhain, which falls on the 31 October.'

'So I have to imagine that yesterday was the 50th anniversary? Is that why you and Mayor Chapman and Judge Owen had to recover the books at all costs?'

Adam Ford shook his head.

'It's not like that. The last rite is dated 31 October 1850 and no more should have been celebrated for the next sixteen years. You must bear in mind that the night of Samhain falls on 31 October of each year, but it is not necessary to recite any rite other than a prayer of thanksgiving or a dedication to those who were dear to you in life and are now no longer there. It is a mysterious night, in which a gap is opened that connects our world to that of the dead, allowing quiet souls to return to visit those close to them. The living leave food and water outside their homes to feed them, along with lighted candles to help them find their way back. The souls refresh themselves, then go into their homes and caress the heads of their loved ones, begging for a peaceful life and a comfortable place for them when the world of the dead drags them along.'

Dorian Bayley understood why in the village the windowsills of many houses had been decorated as small votive shrines.

'The forces that rule the universe, however,' Adam Ford regained, 'cause every 50 years a third dimension to align with the other two, the seat of the kingdom where evil boils up with its army of damned creatures. The days before this event are characterized by strange events: animals become restless, gusts of wind shake the forest and the earth trembles with terrifying thunder. It is only then that we members of the sect are called to celebrate the rite of *Ambactus Danu*.'

'I guess, then, something must have gone wrong this time…'

Dorian Bayley was beginning to understand.

'That's right,' confirmed Adam Ford. 'Vernon Doyle must have opened the book and recited the formula, believing some silly popular rumour that delegates to those formulas the power to confer immortality.'

'Invocation,' observed Dorian Bayley intrigued, 'the book stolen from you contained the formula of the invocation.'

Adam Ford smiled as well, acknowledging the inspector's uncommon intuitive ability.

'The invocation is only the first part of the formula; it is necessary because it would make no sense to recite the next parts, which end with the rejection of the beast into the underworld, if you are not sure that you have found it first.'

The inspector nodded to Ford to stop for a moment. He got up and went through his coat pocket, pulled out a note and showed it to him.

'I must imagine that the rest of the ritual is about apparition, imprisonment and expulsion to the underworld.'

Adam Ford watched him shake his head again.

'This is my son Martin's handwriting.'

'I was almost certain but now I have confirmation as to who put it in my pocket at Vernon Doyle's funeral,' smiled the inspector.

'My son is a little sceptical and that worries me because he's the one who should take my place when I'm gone. He believed that by giving you clues, you could help us find the book. He knew it was vital to me, and he wanted my peace of mind.'

'Let's go back to Vernon Doyle,' the inspector retook over the last parentheses.

'The power of the magic formula lies not only in the words that compose it, but also and above all in being recited by masters initiated in a sacred place, following precise secular rules. Otherwise, there is a risk of altering the balance with which good and evil share existence in this universe. Without any shrewdness, Vernon Doyle limited himself to reading the formula of the invocation from the original text, causing the temporary opening of a gap between ours and the dimension of the underworld, allowing a demon to cross it. Hence the terrible events of the last days. My task, that of Mayor Chapman and Judge Owen, who, together with Nevil Morgan, as you must have understood by now, are the other members of the sect, was to recover the manuscripts at all costs; it was the only way to interrupt this macabre chain of murders. Once she learned of Nevil Morgan's murder, Madame Eleanor made herself available to celebrate the imprisonment formula contained in the text that the inspector was guarding.'

Adam Ford caught his breath. He rearranged the events in his own head and then went on.

'When we wanted to retrieve the manuscript, however, we realized that someone had gone before us; he had entered Nevil Morgan's house and taken possession of the text, throwing us into absolute panic. Thanks to my son Adam, who was able to open doors and locks, we were able to retrieve his personal diary, in which there was a note that immediately attracted our curiosity. The inspector had managed to discover the place where Vernon Doyle had hidden the manuscript and had written it down, perhaps because he wanted to leave a trace of his investigation knowing the danger.'

He beckoned the inspector to open the diary and pointed to a specific page.

'Library, second desk on the left starting from the back wall, under brick with engraved cross,' read aloud Dorian Bayley.

'So, together with the judge and the mayor, in the middle of the night, you thought you'd go and retrieve the book, hoping that the stolen text in Nevil Morgan's house was also hidden there...'

'You were already having me followed, weren't you, Inspector?' Asked Adam Ford no hard feelings.

'Tell me what happened that night,' Dorian Bayley encouraged him, taking the answer for granted.

'We searched the floor of the entire library, under the carpets, moving objects and shelves, lighting every square inch of the surface with lamps, but there was no trace of the brick with the engraved cross. We returned to it in sorrow and disconsolation, but not resigned. We could not leave *Greystone* in mortal danger.'

Dorian Bayley refused to give credence to what Adam Ford believed in and to which, together with characters who were anything but foolish, he had dedicated part of his life. However, the story was precious to him because it dispelled his last doubts and explained, like a perfect cog, the events that still lacked small details.

'What did you do then?'

'I could see that Jacob Young was following me. After your last visit, I feared that you would soon imprison me, thus wiping out the last remnant of hope. I had to evade the officer's surveillance and hide in the mayor's house; if this is a crime, now that everything is over, I am ready to pay without the slightest remorse.'

Dorian Bayley smiled.

'We were groping in the dark until we found out about poor Margaret's murder and the theft of the third book in Judge Owen's house,' Adam Ford continued, 'that night we went back to the library willing to knock over every single tile to find the book cache, but we didn't have to.'

The inspector raised an eyebrow and his face asked a silent question.

'Under a carpet,' Ford said, 'there was one engraved with the symbol of a crucifix. It is likely that, before our inspection, Father Beathan hid the hiding place by turning the tile upside down. We would never have suspected he might have been involved in all this; unfortunately we realised too late that we had underestimated his refined, albeit sick, intelligence. The fact is that, after hiding the third book from us, perhaps in a hurry, he must have positioned it in the right direction again. We put pressure on the sides and the tile, which was just stuck, came away together with the two adjacent ones, bringing to light a secret periphery where we found the three texts. We breathed a sigh of relief; a few hours later we would have had to celebrate the rite but, without those manuscripts, we would have found ourselves facing a ferocious enemy without any defence.'

'What if you had performed the ritual the next day?' Asked Dorian Bayley, intrigued by the story though sceptical.

'Our knowledge does not allow us to predict everything. On the other hand, Inspector, until a few days before, we were unaware of what forces could trigger the recitation of the formula by someone not belonging to the *Ambactus Danu* sect. We have witnessed the terrible power that these texts hide and now that we know the danger generated by their improper use, it will be our responsibility, and that of our successors, to guard them with absolute care.'

The silence was filled with the incredulous and fascinated thoughts of Dorian Bayley.

'Father Beathan,' he sentenced, 'has crossed all ethical boundaries; lured by the promise of a very rich reward in money and driven by a sick mind that has slowly dragged him into madness, he had no scruples about killing to try to achieve his goal. He also involved Vernon Doyle in his criminal plan by exploiting the keeper's complete awe of him, then, when he became a danger, he killed him brutally. Doesn't that strike you as a more credible explanation, Mr Ford?'

Adam Ford spread his arms.

'I don't expect everyone to believe; on the contrary, I am convinced that for *Greystone*'s sake it is better that all this remain confidential, invisible, a simple fantasy story to be told on a cold winter night in the warmth of a fireplace and in the company of friends. But evil has deep roots and its way of acting remains mysterious and unpredictable. This time it has struck by corrupting the soul of a priest, of a man whose goodness was known throughout the village, turning him into a sadistic and bloodthirsty murderer. In this way it has not only succeeded in sowing death, terror and pain, but has blatantly challenged an entire community, showing them how its cruelty mocks those who claim to be its sworn enemy on earth.'

'The question remains why all these explanations have not been given to me before.'

In the inspector's words, there was a sudden vein of resentment which, however, immediately faded into a benevolent expression.

'As you can imagine, we are forced to act in the utmost secrecy; we operate in absolute secrecy, victims of a religious persecution that has lasted for centuries, fed by the high hierarchies of the official church. How could we trust you? Furthermore, our priority was the manuscripts; if the police had recovered them, in all probability, we would not have been able to celebrate the rite of Black Samhain, with consequences impossible to predict. I hate to flee the law, and I acknowledge that I acted illegally, evading capture and withholding information from you. Believe me, Inspector, I am prepared to suffer the consequences, which can never compare to the bloodshed that would have continued to terrorise *Greystone* if we had not been able to perform the ritual last night.'

'There will be no consequence for you, Mr Ford,' reassured Dorian Bayley, 'and rest assured, I will keep your membership of *Ambactus Danu* secret, which, allow me to express my thoughts, has had no influence on the restoration of peace in *Greystone*.'

The fact that the inspector remained firm on his position could only reassure Adam Ford. As much as he was a man of his word, it was always preferable that his interest in the sect, like everyone else's, was limited.

'There's something I'd like to say to you before I wish you a safe return to London.'

'You're welcome.'

'Father Beathan did not know the access to the cave and could never have escaped that way after the murder of Vernon Doyle; unless...'

'Unless what?'

'Someone, or rather something, had guided him to that exit, otherwise impossible to find, as you may have seen for yourself.'

'The only concession I can make to you, Mr Ford, is that the air in this village has something suggestive. In concrete terms, however, I have not noticed anything that cannot be explained by reason or by human endeavour. For example,' he stopped to finish the brandy left in the glass, 'Madame Eleonor herself, after falling into a trance, had informed me that Nevil Morgan's lifeless body was in a dark and cold place. If we try to strip the information from the veil of the theatricality with which it had been given to me and we think that at that moment the most plausible hypothesis was that Inspector Morgan had been murdered, which I was already certain of, it would not have been difficult to transform the result of a simple analysis of the facts into a gift bestowed by a spirit who had got in touch with what you consider a seer.'

On Adam Ford's face was printed a grimace that betrayed the tiredness of a sleepless night. The cemetery attendant got up and Dorian Bayley walked him to the door. They said goodbye like old friends. Before he took his leave, however, Ford stared the inspector in the eye.

'How do you explain that Madame Eleanor had the exact same vision in my presence the day before Nevil Morgan disappeared?'

Without waiting for a reply he wished the inspector good life and walked away wearing his wide woolly hat.

***

Bringing to trial anyone who had hidden a truth in the days of *Greystone* would have meant accusing most of those who resided there, starting with Judge Owen and ending with Darrel Bennet, whose position ranged between different degrees of responsibility. Dorian Bayley was inclined to the least heavy of hypotheses, the one that Bennet himself had made in his last interview before his visit to Father Beathan, culminating in his suicide. Bennet had confessed that he had instructed the priest to find the four texts that Donald Acton had commissioned him, but had asked him to buy them and then sell them to Bennet himself at a very high price, which would have guaranteed Father Beathan a very good margin. Bennet had claimed that he had approached the prelate because he had learned, later found to be unfounded, that the texts were kept in the church library and, secondly, because he had contacts with all the inhabitants of *Greystone,* which would allow him to negotiate the purchase from a privileged position. All this went very smoothly and there was no reason to doubt Bennet's good faith, but then, suspecting that the priest was involved with the murder of Vernon Doyle and the robbery of Adam Ford's house, he preferred to change air, fearing that the clues had led Inspector Bayley on his trail. Not resigned to losing a business of that magnitude, Darrel Bennet had not returned to London, but had taken refuge in nearby *Little Castle*, where a series of auctions and events involving valuable objects and paintings were held, thus achieving the dual purpose of disappearing from the scene and buying some interesting pieces for his collection. He had had no further contact with Father Beathan until the day of Margaret's murder. In fact, shortly before Judge Owen broke into the inspector's office to announce the discovery of poor Margaret's body, Father Beathan had managed to sneak into the basement of the building to inform him that the third book had also been recovered and that only one was missing to obtain the agreed reward. When Judge Owen announced Margaret's death, however, Bennet was convinced that the priest was the murderer and a long shiver of terror ran up his back thinking he might be accused of complicity. At best, the accusation of being the instigator of a murder would have sentenced him to prison for the rest of his life. He had thought about what to do and had come to the conclusion that the game was lost; he would have to tell the inspector the whole truth. After Margaret's murder, however, the hours had become hectic and there was no way to get an interview with him or his officers until the inspector suddenly appeared before he went to arrest Father Beathan.

In the hours leading up to the 12 o'clock departure to Middlesbrough, Dorian Bayley allowed himself one last walk to *Greystone*. He wanted to breathe the air of a village that had returned to life, without fear, without any more chilling questions to ask, but with a terrible memory that would take time to fade and be forgotten. What he did not expect was the demonstration of affection and esteem that every person with whom he had dealt in those days had shown him. *Greystone* was grateful to Inspector Bayley because, beyond all the beliefs that would continue to shape life and relationships between people, he had managed to enter a community with sensitivity and decision, risking his own life in an attempt to restore serenity and peace to all the inhabitants. Now that Nevil Morgan was gone, many would have seen Dorian Bayley as his ideal replacement.

'By now you know things that integrate you into this community and make you the perfect person to replace Inspector Morgan,' Judge Owen told him.

Flattered by those words, Dorian Bayley promised himself he would return as soon as he was discharged from Scotland Yard.

When he looked out the door of George Davies' workshop, the blacksmith was sitting on a stool and was handling a wooden plank.

'I see you're into carpentry too,' Bayley laughed.

'I heard about your departure,' replied the blacksmith, who looked like he was looking for a pretext to postpone his work, 'but first you and I have a mission to accomplish, don't we?' He asked as he took off his work coat and wore a heavy coat.

Dorian Bayley pulled out his watch but George Davies didn't give him a chance to object.

'It'll only take ten minutes, then I'll take you to get your luggage and be your porter to the station. George Davies never forgets who bought him a drink.'

The inspector resigned himself and, together, they got into the carriage that had been entrusted to him for the period of his stay in *Greystone*. The blacksmith had kept his word. At 11.45 a.m. they were on the platform where the train was already waiting; next to the faithful officers Gordon Craig and Jacob Young were Mayor Chapman and Martin Ford, who came to greet him on behalf of the village.

Dorian Bayley hated goodbyes because they were often accompanied by a deep shared sorrow; he had to fight with all his strength not to be gripped by nostalgia, able to tangled up like a hungry snake.

Once the pleasantries were over, he took a seat in the carriage in the company of the small barrel of beer, picked up with the help of the mighty arms of George Davies. He felt tired but satisfied; while the train left the small station he was able to admire for the last time the beauty of *Greystone* covered with snow, with its smoking chimneys and the stone buildings on which the story of a community out of the ordinary was written.

When he was minutes away from arriving at Middlesbrough station he remembered the letter that Adam Ford had given him; he put his hands in his pocket and took it. As sender there was only the name "Madame Eleonor"; he opened it and read the brief contents, written in elementary but easy to understand handwriting.

'Your son Samuel is happy and wishes to see you again.'

He dropped the paper on the floor; he clenched his fists and his arms began to shake as if he were about to explode. He had to use all his self-control to avoid being overwhelmed by memories. The train on which he was traveling, an hour later, would return to *Greystone,* but he would tear up that letter, catch the connection to London, and return to his old life.

Dear reader,

as always we want to thank you for reading our novel: for us writing, as well as being an intense commitment, is a passion that feeds with the hope of making the reader spend a few pleasant hours.

Just because our ultimate goal is to give those who read a positive experience, we would like to ask you the kindness to offer us a couple of minutes to write a short review on Amazon; will serve us authors to have an objective and valuable feedback and will serve future readers who can get an idea of the novel allowing a conscious and targeted purchase. You can also contact us in private for a greeting or for any question you want to ask us. We will always answer with great pleasure. We leave here below our social contacts with the hope to see you soon. Thank you very much.

Francesco Cheynet & Lucio Schina

Instagram contacts:
- francescocheynet
- lucio_schina

Web site: www.schinacheynetlibri.it